In Their Ruin

Joyce Goldenstern

Books by Joyce Goldenstern

The Story Ends—The Story Never Ends
Old Woman and Eel and Other Prose Pieces (chapbook)
Way Stops Americana (chapbook)

In Their Ruin

Joyce Goldenstern

Black Heron Press
Post Office Box 614
Anacortes, Washington 98221
www.blackheronpress.com

ISBN (print): 978-1-936364-44-2
ISBN (ebook): 978-1-936364-45-9

Cover art and design by Bryan Sears. Copyright © 2024 by Bryan Sears.

Author photo copyright © 2023 by Joyce Goldenstern.

Acknowledgments: The title "In Their Ruin" alludes to the Dylan Thomas poem, "I see the boys of summer in their ruin." The prologue line, "An unsolved mystery is a thorn in the heart," is a prompt from Joyce Carol Oates' online Master Class, which she invited her students to use as their own. Thank you to Michele Beaulieux, Sandi Wisenberg and Maureen Connelly for preliminary editing help, and Jerry Gold from Black Heron Press for his editing suggestions.

The "Chester" chapter from Part I was first published in Aji Magazine under the title "Chester in Another Dimension." The first "Samuel" chapter was originally published in Write Launch under the title "Inquisitor."

John, ever after

Prologue

From the journal of Ruth Winters, April 7, 2016:
An unsolved mystery is a thorn in the heart.

None of us, in the end, would be able to solve the mystery of the missing mother, but we pondered and told and remembered the puzzle of her vanishing to mark its significance somewhat beyond the passing day.

How important she must have been to them: a female in a household of males, and the one who knew her sons and taught them their thoughtful manners.

Part One: Before
(1948 – 1968)

See them in the distance, the boys of light and shadow—their deft and graceful movements, dancing to their ruin.

Gladys

She started bringing comic books home to read to her sons: Hank, her oldest son who had complained impatiently that the stories she had first been telling at bedtime were about grown women—Bird Woman, Crying Woman, or Cat Woman (didn't she know any about boys?)—and Samuel, her second son, who had explained patiently that when Hank said he wanted stories about boys who could fly or climb buildings, he was in fact talking about comic books. Gladys knew that reading was her oldest son's worst subject in first grade. Hank, short, wiry, smart and dark-complected like her, but unlike her, with no time for what did not make sense, seemed happy enough with her new approach: He liked the animated drawings, the balloons with asides in them, simple words like Hmm! and Wham!, Argh! and Yikes!, though he pointed out, of course, the stories were not true. Human beings could not fly; super-heroes with superpowers just helped us to think up cool inventions that really could be invented like strong cleats for shoes or aerodynamics for cars.

"What's true," said Samuel who was more attuned to theme and metaphor and who would be among the best readers in class when he got to be in first grade, "is that we should save people in trouble when we can, like the heroes do. That's what the stories are trying to say."

Hank agreed with his younger, but taller, brother yet insisted that it was also very true that we could not really fly without a glider or airplane. Gladys, at that moment, felt proud of her two oldest sons who were polite and thoughtful, and she felt happy with her baby Felix too, who did not quite understand stories yet, but slept peacefully nearby, an uncritical audience, oblivious to conflict and resolution and the elusiveness of meaning and truth.

Gladys herself had trouble remembering the arcs and morals of the stories her mother had told her when she was a child living on the farm. Stories neatly wrapping things up had always bothered her. The vivid images and personalities carried on in her mind, refusing to be contained by moral or neat resolution, attaching themselves to new unrelated situations, twisting and turning their way down a crooked trail blazing through her imagination. The farmhouse on the plains of western South Dakota did not hold many of its own books, but one of her older brothers left behind the *Golden Book of Science* when he joined the U.S. Army Air Corps to fight in World War II. She used its photographs of stalagmites and stalactites as well as the images she remembered from her mother's native stories and Irish stories laced with snatches from an unreturned library book, *Folktales from Many Lands,* to make up stories to entertain her little brother and sister when her mother left her in charge.

When Gladys had children of her own, she lived in Cicero, Illinois, far from where she grew up. She had married a nice man, an intelligent man, but a complex one, and she felt the burden of keeping the household on an even keel. She worked as a bartender and was not always around in the evenings to tell stories, so she made a special effort those evenings that she was at home to tell a bedtime story or read a comic book. Her son Hank had made a good point with his complaint. She realized that she had, at first, been composing stories not particularly suitable for her children, but ones to help her understand her own quandaries.

She continued with the comic books, but sometimes alternated them with stories she made up. Every now and again, much to Hank's consternation, she would slip up and return to stories about women, usually wives or mothers who were really birds or fish or cats and whose domestic lives misfortune touched in one tragic way or another.

Samuel

The first evil thing that Samuel Stone remembered doing in his life happened when he was nine years old. He burned a martyr at the stake.

Of Gladys's three sons, Samuel was the one who listened most intently to Gladys's stories and asked the most questions. He was a practical child who carefully counted his allowance coins, but also a child who appreciated metaphors. For example, when Gladys told the story of the bird woman, Samuel understood that such a woman would not really exist, but still might be worth hearing about. Surely people existed who would like to fly from a troubled or confining situation or who felt out of place in the company of others. He himself once hid in a closet with a jar full of fireflies to watch them light up, so he could accept that Bird Woman might want her privacy in the closet. He had enjoyed being alone and sometimes sat in the front closet even when he did not have a jar full of fireflies.

When Gladys told him another story that she embellished from *Folktales from Many Lands*, of Crying Woman who drowned her own children to punish her husband who had left her and then wandered the riverbank every night calling their names, and who sometimes snatched a village child away to replace those she lost, Samuel listened intently. "I feel sorry for her," he said, "because she's crazy. The story should bring the kids back to life. Stories can do that, right?"

He was the son who asked her if he could be an altar boy. He liked the idea of bread being transformed into the body of Christ, and wine being transformed into the blood of Christ. More than anything, he wanted the responsibility to ring the bell when the transformations

happened. He also liked being able to count the money that the servers
collected after Mass was over.

The day Samuel took on the role of Inquisitor and burned a martyr
at the stake had started out with Samuel, his cousin Junior, and their
playmate Anthony Pietrowski playing in Junior's garage. Junior noticed
that the red Cadillac, usually off limits, was unlocked and the boys
piled into the front seat, Junior in the driver's seat madly rocking the
steering wheel side to side, feigning his expertise as a race car driver,
then Samuel tumbling into the back seat in a move to simulate a shot
stunt man, but then immediately noticing a hump in the vehicle mat
and finding under the mat a knife with a switch blade and an envelope full of 100-dollar bills. Such a find seemed more wondrous, yet
puzzling, than they could imagine. What else might be hidden in the
forbidden red Cadillac?

Junior knew the way to open the trunk and there they found a
beat-up box with a mask, a wig, a revolver, and a long-reach butane
lighter. Now it so happened that Samuel and Hank often frequented
the Joke Store and over the years had bought fake poo, Groucho Marx
glasses with a moustache, a rubber hatchet, a gun that shot a flag, a fake
ID which gave them credentials as gangsters, and a bulbous nose that
honked when you squeezed it. Disguise and trickery intrigued him as
did the ritual at St. Mary of Częstochowa Catholic church in the Hawthorne neighborhood of Cicero where he served as an altar boy. Indeed,
the three playmates lived in a town where tiny shrines to the Virgin
Mary dotted the lawns, while the lawns defined territories claimed by
street gangs; and stores and bars with cash registers, juke boxes, and
slot machines were frequented by parishioners and knights from the
Knights of Columbus while at the same time visited by members of
sinister crews: the sacred and the profane seemed of a piece, and the
just discovered stash in the car a clue to a strange, yet familiar, puzzle.

The long-reach lighter might or might not be of use lighting can in the church. The mask might or might not be worn by a penitent during holy week, the wig might or might not be donned by a Hasidic Jew in a nearby neighborhood—a shot toward the sky from the revolver might welcome in the New Year or signal the Epiphany—or maybe not. Anthony Pietrowski had overheard whispers and fragments of stories about Junior's father that could well lead him to imagine more profane associations, but these hovered murkily and led to questions hard to articulate and matters beyond his apprehension: he knew enough to keep his thoughts and doubts to himself and his mouth firmly shut on such matters.

"We better put everything back, just as we found it," Junior advised. And so, slowly they did, except for the long-reach lighter, which Samuel held in his hands, hesitant to surrender.

"Have you heard of the martyrs?" Samuel asked.

"You mean like Joan of Arc?" Anthony offered.

"Burned at the stake," added Junior.

"We could do it," Samuel cautiously suggested. "I mean just pretend. Just a few flames."

"I don't want to pretend to be a girl," Anthony said.

"You wouldn't have to be Joan of Arc. You could be Geoffrey de Charney from the Knights of the Order of Templar," Samuel replied.

"Why was this guy Jeff burned at the stake?" asked Junior, who respected Samuel's book knowledge.

"Idolatry and sodomy," replied Samuel. "He was accused of worshipping a cat whose head had three faces and mating with said cat, though he was a human man. He was tortured until he confessed."

"Was there any truth to what they said about him?" asked Anthony who didn't know the words idolatry or sodomy.

"I doubt it," said Samuel. "The king of France just wanted his land. The Templars protected pilgrims. They fought in the crusades and believed in God."

"Do you believe in God?" Junior asked.

"Yes, I do," Samuel said. "Of course."

"We can put the lighter back later," Junior said. "But it must be before my father finds out."

"Could a cat really have three faces?" asked Anthony, as the three friends with three distinct faces talked and walked and then rode bikes to the canal and walked their bikes across a truss bridge slicked in spots with leaked drops of oil from all the truck traffic to find a private place that might serve to site a pyre.

*

Here on an embankment: see them in the distance: three boys that long-ago summer, boys of light and shadow with their deft and grace-ful movements, movements now with a driven purpose, throwing twigs in a circle of stones, dancing to their ruin, raising a tree limb as a cross, twining shoe strings round two wrists, wild boys in their futile folly, flaring the sparks blazing the accidental drops of oil, and then moments later the boys panicking, arms flaying, feet stomping as they try to extinguish the blaze and muffle the curdled scream in a martyr's throat, and soon after the sirens rushing the streets to quell the frenzy of the flame burning a field. All a blur now. Full of consequence, but unclear: how had they arrived here? What had prodded them to sum-mon death this summer afternoon?

An ambulance rushed Anthony's charred body to the hospital. A fire hose extinguished the flames. Cops circled around the two remain-ing boys, one who held a long-armed butane lighter in his hand, while nearby the irrevocable evidence: embers smoldering, smoke wafting: burning nostrils, tearing eyes. Sorry would never now be enough. Bless us Father for we have sinned, but how to assess that sin, how to tell it (when all words fail) and calculate its penance, how to sign our foreheads

with the cross: the blood, the berry, the flint, the pitch, the five Hail
Marys, the ten Our Fathers and the one Apostle Creed thrown in for
good measure?

Hank

Sister Immaculata stood before his mother and him and told his mother he did not try hard enough. "He rates very high on his intelligence tests," she said, adjusting her stiff wimple, "but he refuses to learn to read." He wondered if the letters swam before the eyes of Bonnie Dempster the way they swam before his. She did not seem to have to try hard to keep them in order to read aloud in a steady stream with calm and appropriate inflection and expression. Thus, and so, they labeled him as lazy and that was that. They gave him a U—Unsatisfactory—for effort. He kept the hurt and the unruly letters (the U among many others) to himself and at bay, but he sometimes broke out in hives. He did not pray to God, for God was one of their stories.

Somewhat like Huck Finn, Hank Williams Stone took little stock in stories about dead people nor imaginary ones, except cartoons and comics. His mother liked to tell a bedtime story about a mother who was really a bird called a sun gazer who sewed blankets for her children in a closet. He did not argue the impossibility with her. He did not want to hurt her feelings, but his mind wandered to other matters when she told the story. On the other hand, he spent afternoons on Bonnie Dempster's living room floor for several months and listened to her read any story she chose—whether imaginary or not—intrigued by how the puzzling words on the page tripped from her tongue. Reading far above her grade level, she introduced him to Joe and Frank Hardy and to Tom Sawyer and Huck Finn as well as Jo, Meg, Beth, and Amy. Hank liked to have smart girls in his life, but even at age seven, he felt he needed to keep his proper distance to avoid entanglements that would limit him as school limited him, as home rules limited him.

The story of his mother and father seemed foggy and beyond chronology. Mother, Father had been happy enough once in that cloudiness: time upon time. Perhaps his parents had even been in love. He, Hank Williams Stone, had been born into a home of love and lusty attraction. As a preschooler he had trusted his parents.

His trust of him, the father, eroded slowly at first, and as it did, his trust of her grew stronger by default, but that too could be tenuous, for she often chased him with a belt and sternly warned him to obey laws of the land *because of the situation*—not that he ever had broken any. But she, Gladys, his mother was the mother of boys and the sister of them and feared the future of her boys in a rough-and-tumble town. She could not, would never be able to, rescue him from trouble with the law. She would never bail him out—so do not even ever ask her to. He sensed he was not supposed to pry into what exactly *the situation* was—so he did not. It was when she admitted that she herself was Santa Claus that he stopped believing in God. From then on, he knew he was on his own in a vast unpredictable universe. His first lesson in physics (a subject that would later beckon him to its wonders): the concept of randomness.

*

One October his mother made chicken soup as he sat on a kitchen stool and watched her. She was not always a mother who stayed at home to cook and sew and clean. She worked as a bartender at the race-track. So, he shadowed her, as much as he could, for that month that she stayed home. He asked her about a silver ring that she sometimes wore on her right middle finger, prettier, he thought, than the gold band she wore on her left ring finger.

"My aunt gave it to me before I left the farm and came to Illinois. I think she was asking me to forgive her because she beat me once. She blamed me for something that was not my fault. I still can't forgive her, though I think the ring is pretty. The seven points of the star represent seven ancestors that went separate ways. The webbing in the middle means they are still connected," his mother told him, showing him the ring up close and pointing out its parts. "It is pretty," his mother repeated, "but I don't wear it often because it reminds me of a sad time."

"What did she beat you for?" Hank asked, finding the first part of her explanation more compelling, now, than the ring itself.

"A wild boar gored her daughter, my cousin Sherry. We were playing together in a field. That pig killed my cousin. I suppose my aunt wanted someone to blame, so she blamed me," his mother told him matter-of-factly.

Hank fell silent, continuing to watch her make the chicken soup. He would remember the outlines of the recipe for the rest of his life and even as he grew old would duplicate it with carrots and parsnips and celery.

During that month, he often found her pedaling the sewing machine, long pieces of silky red and black cloth and black lace being pieced together. Last year she designed a Hank Williams outfit for him on that same sewing machine: a white jacket with pressed on musical notes, a cowboy hat, boots, a signature necktie, cufflinks for the white shirt. But this year she had another idea. He did not object when at Halloween his mother decided he must dress as a Spanish senorita and wear the dress that she had fashioned. He trusted his mother that much and lacked disdain of the opposite gender that much, at that time, but did cry out in protest when he was announced the winner for best costume and was about to be awarded a story-book doll: "I'm a boy," he cried, tearing off his black veil. "I don't want a doll." And so they gave him a holster with a cap gun instead, signaling him a cowboy with a mission to shoot Indians. He liked that better and did not consider, at that moment, that his own heritage might hold traces of Cherokee, a story that he had found interesting when his mother mentioned it, but not one his take on the world measured or weighed. He identified with the cowboy.

One day during the summer Hank finished first grade, his father, who usually loomed a distant figure locked up in his basement office, took him and Samuel fishing at Maple Lake in a forest preserve not far from Cicero. They dug up night crawlers before dawn, and he outshone both his father and his brother in finding them. Here was his mastery: he could thread a worm on a hook effortlessly; he could cast a line with no instruction for he had seen others do it and had practiced the flicks of his wrist alone in his room; he could reel a sunfish in and unhook a hook from the roof of its mouth and steady its struggling in his small hand; he could steel himself against the waves of compassion that a cold-eyed struggling fish might elicit, but did, in the end, prefer to return the fish to the water if he could, and this preference did not mark him a sissy but came with a perfectly respectable name: catch and release. From then on, he favored the lake and forest and forsook the classroom; he delighted in the open fields and the fishing waters and scorned the enclosed reading circle of those deigned slow or unpromising readers. He should now and could and would read the forest, the river, the fields with confidence and competence.

And then the uncles on the mother's side in South Dakota during vacations finished the lessons in lake fishing and imparted other lessons about river fishing and ice fishing and hunting and trapping and the ways of nature and the importance of filleting fish with very sharp knives that allowed no waste or rough edges, and eating all that one found on one's plate. They took him, the eldest but the shortest and the most high-strung and Samuel, two years younger but a head higher, on as charges, for the voices his father began hearing in his head kept him more firmly than ever locked in his basement office where he worked all day placing bets on horses and on numbers, which kept him from his sons, his family, and prevented him from returning with them to Maple Lake.

And then the other uncles, those on the father's side, most of whom were not real uncles at all but liked to be called so as they handed over shiny silver dollars to him and Samuel for being upright and respectful little men. Uncle Elbows, Uncle Joey Doves, Uncle Laddie and Uncle Mosquito, the latter being an uncle who had shot an annoying mosquito, in a moment of frenzied anger, with a pistol. Slowly he discerned their stories and their status and the genesis of their peculiar names. Uncle Joey Doves, for example, was his father's boss, who once got arrested after a hunting trip for bringing too much game (dead doves) over the state border. Elbows and Mosquito were his father's business associates. Uncle Laddie was married to his father's sister, so he should, unlike the others, be considered a genuine Uncle, if not a blood one. Uncle Laddie's son, another Ladimer, but called Junior, was a hemophiliac and someone whom Hank's mother Gladys took under her wing and made him her own sons' playmate—but carefully the play must proceed, no roughhousing.

And so he found himself in a shiny red Cadillac riding shot gun with Junior by his side and Uncle Laddie at the helm, the diamond on his uncle's little finger sparkling as he turned the steering wheel. Suddenly, seemingly apropos of nothing, Junior burst into tears—crying and confessing and blubbering so neither he nor Uncle Laddie could understand his offense or dismay and had to painstakingly decipher the jumbled words. Hank's German Shepherd Major had run from the yard earlier that day and Junior was admitting that he had forgot to shut the gate. "If that's the worst thing you ever do, you have nothing to worry about, Son," Uncle Laddie said, patting his son's knee.

"What is the worst thing you have ever done, Daddy?" Junior whimpered after a pause, as his sobs waned and he started to calm down. And what then happened next implanted Junior's question forever in Hank's mind. What happened next was nothing. At least for a moment, a silence enveloped the three of them. Uncle Laddie's face turned white. Finally, he spoke in an ominous tone, "Maybe you'll find out someday, Junior," he said, his voice solemn and even, his eyes steady on the road ahead.

Hank would not register Uncle Laddie's white face and strange words until years later, for at that moment his own capacity for evil struck him dumb and set his nerves on edge as he himself considered the worst things he had ever done, as his brother Samuel would do a few years later after he ignited a martyr—the first of many such considerations, both before their mother left and again later, years after his mother left them and neither he nor Hank would any longer have her to trust and steady them.

The worst things Hank would do were entangled with his little brother Felix, whom he loved and whom he failed, who would be the bane of his and of Samuel's existence for many years—and then upon his death, their great sorrow forever.

Felix

"Don't be a hamster brain," Hank told Felix. And Felix tried not to be, but he was just a little kid, four years old with brothers eight and ten years old, brothers who got to go fishing in the pond and river, and who got to look for the tails of, not hamsters, but pocket gophers, with the uncles and not only that but also got to run wild outdoors, while he stayed indoors with his grandmother during that extended summer visit to South Dakota in 1960.

His grandma fascinated and disappointed Felix. He had heard she might be a Cherokee, but she did not conform to the Indians he saw on the television shows he watched back home in Cicero, nor to the chief he saw standing next to a teepee at the Wisconsin Dells, an old man with a feathered headdress who had answered his trepidatious "How" with a raised hand and a solemn face into which Felix stared, trying to solve a mystery he could not articulate.

Grandma wore tennis shoes, not moccasins. Sometimes she drank "Spirits," which she poured into a thermos cap from a thermos bottle. She knew how to hold a blade of grass between her thumbs, lift it to her lips and make it whistle. She confirmed the rumor, when he asked, of a great-great-grandmother running off. She told him she had escaped from the Dwight mission in Arkansas to start their family in South Dakota, but Grandma was quite sure she got her own dark skin from Irish ancestors who danced with Spanish sailors.

She gave him a pile of colorful buttons to sort. "If I were a painter," she said, "I would paint the wind green and the sound of a bubbling brook a light blue, the blue of a cerulean warbler. I would use many paintbrushes: Coarse ones made from the hairs of horse tails and fine ones made from the hairs of a gopher." Her husband and his grandpa, Gramps O'Brien, once worked in a button factory. The buttons in Grandma's collection had no holes to thread. "They are highly *irregular*," she told him and if he were good, if he behaved properly, she might bequeath them to him. Sometimes she told him the story about a man within whose body lived two battling wolves and sometimes the one about a boy named Mouse who was a painter whose brushes grew into colorful flowers, and the one similar to, but not quite the same, as one his mother told, about a wife who was really a bird and another one similar to one his mother told, but not quite the same, about a wife who was really a cat. She also told stories about the wee men dressed in green, one of which helped a dark princess who could not speak.

Sometimes Grandma gave him treats, either strawberries mixed with honey or iceberg lettuce sprinkled with sugar. The strawberries and lettuce came from her garden, and on occasion she would take him with her to pick strawberries, which could be fun, but when he saw Hank and Samuel playing with the hose in the distant yard, he thought they probably were having even more fun. "They are diverting the gophers from the garden," his grandma said. But he had no idea what she meant.

Gramps O'Brien owned a Springfield rifle, which his father, Felix's great-grandfather, had used in Cuba during the Spanish-American War. This was quite interesting, and even Hank and Samuel thought so. Someday Grandpa would get the required gunpowder and load and shoot it or so he had promised, and they, the three brothers, hoped he would keep the promise. Felix also secretly hoped his grandpa might *bequeath* the rifle to him—definitely an incentive to behave properly, to be good. Felix knew that Samuel, the middle child and Felix's sometime rival, also wanted the rifle, and Felix often day-dreamed that Grandpa would say, "I am sorry Samuel, but Felix will get the rifle

when I die. I have already *bequeathed* it to him." And Samuel's expect-
ant face would cloud with disappointment.

*

"Please do not whine when you say *please,*" his grandma told him at
least once a day. "Try not to sound like a beggar." He had been saying
"please" a lot to Hank because he wanted to tag along with his brothers
as they collected gopher tails. They kept them in a Mason jar on top
of a dresser in the dining room. Later they turned them in at the post
office for a bounty at a nickel a tail. When he was lucky, Hank would
give him at least one nickel, so he would have candy money when the
uncles took everybody to town in a pick-up truck. Samuel seldom gave
his money away even if he had more tails than Hank ("please" would
be of no use there), but with one nickel from Hank (who could seem
stern, but who, always in the end, was the softer touch), Felix would
buy three black licorice wheels and two Mary Janes. Felix imagined
that the gophers lost their tails the way a snake loses its skin or a deer
its antlers or he his baby teeth and that he might find them in the fields
on the ground, camouflaged by leaves and seeds and fallen stalks and
debris, if only Hank would agree to take him.

Felix tried to amuse himself with the buttons and the daydreams
of the Springfield rifle and conversations with his grandma. "Did the
runaway great-great=grandmother carry a tomahawk?" Felix asked,
hoping for the best, but his grandma didn't think so. Her heavy sigh
suggested that she found his curiosity about the past perplexing, not
only because of his misconceptions but also because of her own gaps
in understanding.

Sometimes Felix wished the summer over. He missed his mother.
She was home in Cicero, working at the racetrack, making overtime
wages in the summer months, so his brothers would have tuition to go

to Catholic school and so he would too when the time came. He was quite sure his mother loved him the best. Last year, on a visit to the farm, Felix had wandered into a pigpen, fell into a water trough and almost drowned. One of his uncles rushed mouth-to-mouth respiration, while his mother screamed hysterically and his grandmother tried to calm her by slapping her face. But she was not comforted until she held him in her arms and he opened his eyes. "I could never lose you," she told him. "Oh, the damn pigs again!" Felix felt fine and had no idea what she was talking about but was glad for the attention. Afterward, she would often ruff the sandy hair on his head and kiss his forehead and call him "Bugs."

Hank first called him "Bugs" and now so did most everyone. He had enjoyed finding roly-polies and spiders in the basement back home and now he helped Grandma pick off jeweled swallowtail caterpillars from infested parsley. "I can see why they call you Bugs," Grandma praised him when he showed her a coffee can full of brilliantly green caterpillars with yellow dots bundled together in a swarming mass. Grandma set them loose on the prairie, saying they would like Queen Anne's lace as much as they did her parsley.

*

That basement in Cicero where he caught spiders and roly-polies was full of telephone jacks with wires that went into his father's office. The neighbor kids who hung around the basement harbored some jealousy: the kids in Felix's family were the only ones in the neighborhood each with a phone to his name, and they had a colored television set and an outdoor swimming pool. How come they got to be so rich? Their house was so big that they rented the second floor to Mexicans.

Having befriended a Mexican horse trainer with a ten-year-old daughter at the racetrack, his mother insisted they rent to them when their Polish tenants moved out. She thought the race-track bunk house ill suited for the daughter Marisol who was so pretty that Samuel and many of the other boys in the neighborhood pursued her, though some of them had been warned by their parents to avoid her, and she showed no interest in any of them (except him, whom she affectionately called Mr. Bugs and whose shoes she sometimes stooped down to tie, looking up afterward to flash her beautiful smile). She swung one of her long thick braids saucily over her shoulder and then the other one over her other shoulder and silently marched to school with a heavy school bag on her back, staring straight ahead without meeting their eyes, and in the late afternoons studied earnestly on the back steps alone. Felix and his brothers were a bit jealous of their mother's solicitude toward the girl. Felix started to worry that his mother might have preferred to have her third child be a daughter. She advised her sons to be nice to Marisol, so one day the three of them stood at the bottom of the back stairs and asked her why she studied so much, and she told them that she planned to be a lawyer when she grew up. They were about to ask her more questions, but after she answered their first question, she opened a book and started reading it, thus ending the conversation and silently dismissing them, though he lingered behind when his brothers wandered off. He sat silently on the bottom step, happy just to be near her while she studied.

The phones, which rang all day long, really were part of his father's business, belonging to the boys in name only. His father would stay holed up in the office for days at a time. One day when he walked out, his hair was all white. "I think he dyed it," Hank told Felix. But Samuel was sure his father had had a terrible shock. He had once read a story of a martyr whose hair turned white before he was beheaded. When they asked their mother, she would only say, "Your father's a very sick man. Sometimes he hears voices. He's mentally ill and may need to go away for treatment." They didn't know what to make of her words. Her words didn't seem to explain the white hair very well at all.

*

Now Hank was drinking water from a hose in Grandma's front yard. He had finally and reluctantly agreed to find gopher tails with Felix, but Felix wondered why he had unwound the hose and was not heading out toward the prairie to look for the discarded tails. If Hank was thirsty, couldn't he drink a glass of water in Grandma's kitchen? In fact, as he drank, Hank considered whether to let his little brother help him collect from the traps that he and Samuel and the uncles had set in the fields or show him the way they captured gophers by drowning them out in the front yard. He decided on the latter, in part because Samuel was collecting in the field and had let Hank know in no uncertain terms that Felix was too little to help and could not tag along.

"I'll show you how to find the holes and plug them up," Hank said, wiping cold water from his chin. Felix wondered what good that would do, but he knew enough not to press the matter or ask questions lest Hank decide he was too much trouble and change his mind about letting him help find the tails. "We will just leave one escape hole open like right here. And this one over there will be our entry hole. I'm going to turn the water up real strong and you put the hose into the entry hole when I say ready." Hank walked over to the escape hole with a rock in his hand, and although confused by what was going on, Felix stuck the hose in the entry hole on cue, trying to be careful not to squirt himself with the forceful water.

As Felix watched Hank hovering over the escape hole, his arms outstretched, an uneasy feeling slowly overcame him along with the terrible dawn of understanding. He screamed when he saw Hank grab a gopher as it emerged from the escape hole. Felix sank to his haunches, wailing and covering his eyes, but peeking slightly with spread fingers when Hank hit the gopher's head with the rock, and he began to sob uncontrollably when Hank took a pocketknife from his pocket and cut off the gopher's tail. Hank was so focused on his work that he did not hear the protest or notice his little brother's distress until he held the bleeding tail up in the air for Felix to see.

"Hey," he said. "What's the matter? You can have the tail. You'll get a nickel for it from Mr. Tooley at the post office." He walked over to his brother, remembering that his grandma had warned that Felix was too young to hunt gophers and also remembering his own initial distaste for the process and how he had somehow found determination to brace himself, to suppress compassion and to learn to feign indifference in part to win his uncles' approval and in part to earn the bounty. "Don't be a hamster brain," he said, gently putting a hand on Felix's shoulder, his casualness belying the concern that Felix heard in the slight quiver in his voice. "Come on, Bugs. It's only a gopher."

Gladys

Beth Anne, one of the 26 girls, told her that Chester was an accountant and so did not dance. Gladys had never known that accountants did not dance before. But then she had come to urban life from a faraway farm and each day brought surprises. She had asked Beth Anne about Chester before Gladys herself was a 26 girl, right when she first started coming to the Club to drink and to dance and to relax after her shift at Western Electric. She had chosen Beth Anne to ask because Beth Anne had freckles on her nose and seemed friendly.

"He keeps the books," Beth Anne added.

"But why does he work at night right here at the Club?"

Beth Anne shrugged her shoulders. "It probably makes it easier for his bosses to talk to him," she said. "Haven't you noticed them marching in and out of the backroom?"

Beth Anne must have let it be known that Gladys was interested in Chester. It was his silent watchfulness that had sparked Gladys's curiosity. A few nights later he came out of the backroom and somewhat shyly offered to buy her a drink. He awkwardly told her that he thought she was pretty in an unusual way. She took his remark as a compliment because she felt the same way about her looks. He continued to come out each evening. He did not seem to mind if she danced with others, since he himself did not know how. "I can teach you to dance," she offered.

"Believe me, you couldn't," he smiled. "It'd be a disaster." She usually did not trust men who did not dance, but he did not seem stiff or repressed, only shy. Since he had work to do, he never could stay to talk for very long. After a few weeks, he asked her to meet him in the back after the bar closed so they would have more time to talk and then that became their routine.

Chester would hold her hand at a small table and speak solemnly. Only a small lamp in the corner lit the room as they sat alone in the deserted club. Even the cleaning crew had gone home. He did not try to kiss her. He seemed to want to explain something to her. They spoke in hushed tones for no reason other than it would have seemed boisterous to disturb the eerie quiet that had descended on such a usually very noisy place. One night as they sat there holding hands, he spoke of his job. He let go of her hand for a moment to show her something. He showed her columns of figures in two ledgers. At the time she did not understand what she was looking at. She was only 18 and had lived her entire life on a farm. Years later she decided that he wanted her to know that his job involved cheating, illegality.

Another night, he spoke of his parents' insanity. The small lamp cast quivering shadows on the wall as he spoke. She followed them: the shadows more than the words. She and he were still holding hands. They still had never kissed. He was not very much older than she was, and yet in some ways he seemed much older. He owned his own house. He had an important job. The way he spoke and the things he spoke about made him seem experienced and wise. She could not always properly chart the flow of his conversation. Was he worried she would be frightened by his parents' insanity? Is that what he was saying? And why was he telling her so much about his family?

He told her that his parents and older sister had emigrated from Austria after World War I. Their passports listed their nationality as Austrian though ethnically they were Polish—they spoke Polish, hardly any German. His mother was pregnant with him. His parents hoped for a boy and a new start in America, but were afraid that they might find lingering prejudice, hard feelings about Austria's role in World

War I. When they arrived, they changed their surname Stoń to Stone to assimilate better. His father soon found a job in the railroad yards, unloading boxcars. But it had been impossible to erase the past and start brand new.

Gladys knew enough about storytelling to figure he must be working up to the part about insanity, the announced theme of the night. She felt he had a strange way of courting her, but she waited patiently. He had told her, "I want to lay all my cards on the table." She had looked down at the small table in front of her when he said this, as though she were trying to study his cards. He needn't have worried she would be upset about his parents' insanity. That was all so very long ago. Besides, she already knew something about being crazy.

When Gladys was a little kid, she had seen a wild pig gore and then eat her cousin. Afterward, she stopped eating meat and stopped speaking for a year, hoping to disappear. After her aunt blamed her and beat her, she tried several times to run away from home but was always found and dragged back. One day, she heard her older brothers discussing her condition. She heard the words "crazy" and "loony". They, too, spoke in hushed tones. She wondered why. She stood near them as they talked. She could still hear them. Maybe her desire to disappear was working—or maybe they thought she was going deaf, and if they lowered their voices, she would not hear. She was not going deaf. She was not deaf, only dumb.

Chester probably knew about many things she didn't know about, but going crazy wasn't one of them.

*

Gladys hated the farm. At age 18 she had the right to leave. She was going to visit her brother in the military in Illinois. She vowed she would never return—a matter of survival: she believed this not so much in her mind as in her churning gut. Years later, she sent her sons to stay at the farm for months at a time, not because she believed they would find wholesomeness in the country air, but because she needed a rest.

Her brother Larry, who was stationed at the Great Lakes Naval Academy in 1948 when she visited him, had told her that Western Electric at the Hawthorne Works in Cicero was hiring women on the assembly line. She was hired and told that even if she married, she could stay on and work; if she had a child, they would provide maternity leave.

Everyone told her she was lucky to have a job with such good benefits. But she didn't like the job. In the evenings after work, she'd go to the Chilee Club to relax and that is where she began to work as a "26 girl" and later as a bartender (a job rare for a woman in Cicero and totally forbidden in Chicago), first just one or two nights a week, but later full time, leaving Western Electric with all its benefits behind. As a 26 girl, she kept score for a Chicago dice game called "26." Charting the rolling dice, chatting with customers, and then, in time, pouring them drinks or serving them a sandwich, was more congenial to her than standing silently on an assembly line, putting together printed circuit boards with cotton in her ears to block out the noise of the roaring machines.

True, sometimes a customer might find her complexion a shade too dark or her looks hard to categorize and ask where she was from. She knew they were implying that she was not an ordinary American, but she would just laugh and joke and say "South Dakota originally" and move on to another customer. But in 1950, seven months before Hank was born, when a mob drove a black family out of town, Gladys took the events to heart. She could no longer easily smile or shrug her shoulders when someone commented on her looks or gender or lively personality. Her nerves on edge, one evening she threw a glass of beer at a drunk who called her a dusky minx." Her boss, Jack Viani, did not admonish her though, as he smoothed over the altercation. He wiped the customer off with a towel and brought him a club soda and told him to stick with club soda: he had drunk too much alcohol. Like her, Jack was a Hank Williams' fan, and besides, he liked her. She was a nice lady. She had spunk. He put a nickel in the jukebox to play Williams' version of "Tennessee Waltz" and waltzed Gladys away from the scene.

*

Even after she married Chester, his job still mystified her: keeping two sets of books for three clubs and then later placing bets on the telephone. Slowly she began to understand that her husband's work depended on his sister's husband Ladimer. She was polite to Ladimer when Chester invited him to the house, but she secretly harbored a distaste for him. His pinky ring studded with diamonds, his gold tooth implanted in his crooked smile, the menacing look unexpectedly darkening his face all added to her suspicion and disgust.

And so she was not pleased that it had been Ladimer that came to the rescue when Anthony was burned and Junior and Samuel were arrested. When Samuel came home with Ladimer from the police station, he looked as though he had been beaten, and he smelled of smoke. She was not sure who had beaten him or even if he had been beaten. Did he still need to be punished at home? Chester never disciplined their sons—he left that to her. But seeing the sorry state of her son, she could not bring herself to lash him with a belt, the way her aunt had once lashed her after the boar attack had killed her cousin, though Gladys in that instance had been blameless in a way she was quite sure Samuel was not. Samuel stood silent at first. Sobs muffled his first utterances of explanation.

Ladimer said he would make all the problems go away. And he did. He paid the hospital bill and the bills for follow-up visits; he diverted any legal problems. Unfortunately, he could not "fix" scorched flesh. In time, however, Anthony's burns, though painful, were not deep and would heal with little scarring. She sent Samuel to visit him in the hospital and to apologize, but after a week of daily visits and apologies, she gave in to Samuel's reluctance and sent Hank, who had a gift for cheering up the downtrodden.

"How many times do I have to tell him I am sorry?" Samuel had complained. "It was his idea too."

"Are you sure about that?" his mother asked skeptically. Her second son had read more than his friends had and had more complicated ideas in his head than they had. He led his tribe of buddies through the neighborhood, sometimes toting a long stick for a spear. Remembering the possibility of a Cherokee ancestor and one of the few Spanish words he knew, Hank had nicknamed Samuel *El Jefe* because he was tall and commanding. Samuel had inherited the high cheekbones and flaring nostrils of Gladys's Dakota brothers. "Never forget what might have happened," she told her second son. "You might've killed someone or ruined a human life." Fortunately, Samuel had not killed anyone, but Anthony stopped playing with him and Junior when he returned home from the hospital, and Gladys wondered if the incident had indeed affected his life as the boar incident had affected hers, had made her less trusting, had made her more eager to run away, to start anew and try to forget past troubles.

After Ladimer let her know that he had paid the bills (and the bribes), she managed to say, "Thank you, Ladimer." But her wariness of him tarnished her gratitude. Meanwhile, Samuel was becoming very introspective. Sometimes when his mother found him sitting silently on the front stoop, his chin resting in his hands, she yearned to know what he was thinking. But he just wanted to be left alone. And so she left him to brood on the front steps.

*

Chester was calling. Chester needed her attention. The voices that troubled him at various times had been troubling him again recently. If she spoke to him very softly, she could calm him. Even if his rantings made no sense, she would reply to them as though they made perfect sense, responding not briefly but with lengthy and intoning exposition and explanations. If she carried on these conversations with him for a long time, he would fall asleep. She had learned this technique through trial and error, but it exhausted her. So after she calmed him one night, she sat in a rocking chair alone to collect her own turbulent emotions. Her thoughts drifted to the long-ago "courtship" talks she had had with Chester in the backroom at the Chilee Club.

"You know I might end up a koo-koo case, a loony tune," Chester had said. "My father went crazy and so did my mother." He hesitated then, before he said, "I had to leave the army in 1944. I didn't want to. I was discharged from the army before the War was over. I suffered from shellshock." His words did not scare her. Their intimacy calmed her, and she continued to listen with equanimity.

He told her that his father, haunted by tortures that he had suffered during the first World War, threatened for years to take his own life and finally did once the Great Depression hit and he lost his job—he took his life by inhaling carbon monoxide, leaving his body draped over a car seat of the Ford coupe the family had acquired before Black Friday. Chester found him in the garage. Soon after, his distraught mother admitted herself to a psychiatric institution, seeking rest and quiet. He had only been 11 at the time. His upbringing fell upon his older sister Angela, who soon after her mother left, married Ladimer.

As Gladys remembered the conversation, she realized how oblivious she had been to obvious warnings. At the time, any worries he had voiced seemed to her surmountable. She could make him smile when she smiled or when she touched his arm. And even though he did not dance, she could make his eyes sparkle with approval when she danced, no matter who her partner. She now marveled how her love for him had been mingled with her own sense of erotic power over him and with her own confusion that allowed her to think love or lust could prevent any catastrophe. She wished Chester could solemnly take her hand again now and talk to her seriously. She longed to confer with him, or anyone sympathetic and sane, as a fellow adult about the boys, about finances, about home repair, about existential despair.

*

About a year after Ladimer cleared up the mess with Anthony, he made arrangements for Chester "to go away" awhile for help. She agreed, seeing no choice, only wishing that Ladimer was not involved in the decision. She had to borrow some money from him to get through the time without Chester's income.

Chester was gone for a year. When he came back after a year, he seemed serene, the commanding voices that had been ruling his life quelled. She allowed herself to hope, to hang new drapes in the dining room, to cook a turkey dinner for Thanksgiving, to invite her brother Larry to the dinner, to make love to Chester that holiday night.

She and Chester started having nightcaps in the evenings. They held hands and laughed together again for a time, which provided a retreat from her worries about Samuel and Hank who were now becoming adolescents as the neighborhood was becoming more dangerous. But soon she came to regret the nightcaps. Chester had gone beyond them and was drinking much of the day. She was no doctor, but she was sure liquor had something to do with her husband's madness. Soon his voices began to whisper again. Within a year the voices grew louder, leaving her with a cold heart and a mind scrambling for a workable strategy. And so that summer of 1964, she moved Hank and Samuel down into the basement, the space that Chester, too delusional to work, had deserted.

*

Her older boys experimented with tobacco and alcohol, she was sure. Maybe even marijuana. Each a leader—Hank, short, dark, and sinewy, and Samuel, tall, light-skinned, and majestic—her two sons patrolled the streets separately with their respective neighborhood gangs—no guns, no knives—but still, the neighborhood had its dangers. Just thinking what might have happened to Anthony Pietrowski, now three years after the martyr incident, still terrified her.

She told Hank and Samuel. "Make the basement into a hangout for your friends. If you drink alcohol, do it here. Smoke, if you want. This will be your place. Hank can take the bed in the office and Samuel the couch by the window. You can invite girls. You can gamble and swear and party. But do it here." Surely, they were safer indulging in these vices at home than on the street.

But, weary, she did not watch them. She did not keep an eye… She only hoped for the best. She closed the basement door and the door to her room when she inhabited the house, which was less and less often. She worked extra shifts. She still owed Ladimer 1,000 dollars and continued to borrow from him even as she tried to repay him.

She would have come home gladly after work to face her problems if she had seen any possible way to solve them, but she had so many and such tangled and impossibly knotted ones. She stayed late at the bar with friends instead. One night and then another and another. She would return home from time to time, often forgetting to stop to buy groceries to stock the empty shelves. Once home, she tried to find her composure amidst dust and dirt, amidst unscoured sinks and dirty toilets, amidst piles of bills, strewn clothes, unmade beds, and unwashed dishes. The color television no longer worked but blared static and flashed colorful patterns. The water in the neglected swimming pool displayed a murky yellow. No one aerated it or changed the chlorine. The boys, no longer wanting to swim in it, threw in carp and catfish they caught in a creek, perhaps thinking the bottom feeders might clean things up or might multiply and provide a backyard fishing hole.

And where was her little boy? Her baby Felix (now nine years old, but still her baby). Spying him on the living room floor, scattered games and scratched phonograph records all about him, she knelt down and swept him in her arms, drew him to her and gently removed the thumb from his mouth (a regression she had just begun to notice). She sang and danced with him,

> *They'll hug you and kiss you and tell you more lies than cross lines on a railroad or stars in the skies. So come all you maidens and listen to me. Never place your affections on a green willow tree, for the leaves they will wither and the roots they will die. You'll all be forsaken and never know why.*

Thus, she feebly tried to invite a moment of harmony into her life, to garner maternal consolation. But all of a sudden, just when she thought she may have achieved a brief semblance of peace, a temporary stay against confusion, a transitory comfort through touch and song, Chester was screaming her name, demanding that she come to him immediately.

Chester

Chester stood naked before a stand-up mirror and contemplated mathematical reiteration and the fourth dimension. Standing before the mirror provided him with a tenuous link to the reality he was leaving behind, for the reverse image in the glass, though mysterious, was in accordance with the laws that governed that real world. Once, years before, it had occurred to him that it would be uncanny to have a mirror-identical twin, so that when they looked in the mirror together each could see his true image in the other's image, not just his own reverse image. Now, however, that wish to see his true image had come true and was driving him mad, for he saw his true image in many places.

For example, he might look out the window and see an exact replica of himself walking down the street or he might hear a voice tell him to look up from the mirror to a high corner in the room, and there he would find his other true self perched like an angel. He understood this to mean that he was losing his individuality and was becoming part of a pattern, the same type of pattern one got by charting imaginary numbers with real numbers and squaring some of them to show a complex number pattern on graph paper: bubbles reproducing, crowding together until they became foam or a dragon curve turning in on itself in the endless feedback of chaos with colorful embellishment and precise duplication. He saw such images clearly in his mind, repeating and repeating, zooming in and zooming out.

Once for a period when Hank was nine or ten, by which time Hank very seldom even spoke to Chester, indeed, avoided him at all costs, Chester found a way to draw him into a conversation through items of mathematical interest. One day he sat at the dining room table with a telephone book opened before him at the white pages. He showed Hank the column of telephone numbers on the right-hand side and told Hank he would add them in his head, which he proceeded to do and within a minute or two came up with the enormous sum.

Of course, Hank had no way he could readily check his father's gigantic claim, so he asked him to do the same with only five rows, which Chester did in a few seconds. When Hank checked and found his father's sum correct, he deliberately muffled his wonder so as not to let his father think he was impressed with him.

Another time, Chester introduced Hank to the concept of a Mobius strip: a strip with width and height but due to a twist, only one surface. Hank had to admit the phenomenon amazed, but strictly the phenomenon, not the teacher, impressed him. When Chester talked about the Klein bottle, a curvature with width and height and depth, but only one surface due to a mysterious twist that one had to imagine being possible in the fourth dimension, Hank seemed to understand the problem and even took a paper towel tube and practiced the twist (albeit approximately, since he could not inhabit the fourth dimension), but he did this alone, away from Chester's supervision. Samuel, on the other hand, showed some respect for his father's knowledge and savant abilities, but not any real interest in trying to understand them. Chester barely acknowledged Samuel's appreciation but continued to long for Hank's approval, for he could see that Hank had inherited some of his obsessions and unique gifts.

Chester now stood without any clothes on because he was finding it harder and harder to attend to hygiene and daily tasks like dressing and making the bed and eating food. He knew that he should take a shower, but taking a shower meant one not only had to remove one's clothes, but also find a washcloth and towel and soap, run the water, adjust the temperature, enter the shower stall, and so forth. To find a clean towel and washcloth meant one would have to wash clothes and then hang them out to dry. In order to wash clothes, one needed to find the laundry detergent and fill the washer with water and soap and dirty clothes, turn on the agitator, and then rinse the clothes, wring them and hang them out to dry. For one thing, he was not one, he was many, so why should he be expected to do what one must do? And where was his wife who was supposed to help him?

Over the course of two days, Chester had managed to remove all his clothes in preparation for a shower. (He found it both mildly alarming and humorous to see from the window his true image walking down the street below with no clothes on.) He had yet to gather the washcloth and towel and soap. He smelled bad, even to himself. And yet a sense of necessity did not propel him; rather, it led him to find relief through distraction.

He began to heed voices telling him that he now needed to contemplate the finite and the infinite. Before him spread a seaside beach: finite in area, but infinite in its parameters. He found a tape measure in Gladys' sewing drawer and dropped with it to his hands and knees to measure each irregular jotting along the shoreline to find the parameter, but the voices told him he must do more. He also must measure each granule on a grain of sand, a task that could go on forever and ever and for which he must find a new measuring tool. The tape measure wasn't working too well. He was busy at work when he suddenly stopped and erected his naked body from the floor to its full height: five feet eight inches. It had occurred to him with great urgency that he wanted to tell Hank about the infinite in the finite.

However, he had not seen Hank for at least a month, and he avoided going down to the basement, even avoided going to the basement door, for he did not want to be reminded that he no longer earned money, that he no longer had an office in the basement. He didn't want to admit that Gladys was the breadwinner now. He knew his brother-in-law had removed the telephones he had used in the basement office; he knew that Hank had taken over the office room for a private bedroom and that Samuel and Hank ruled there now.

He was supposed to leave them alone and keep an eye on his youngest son, Felix, while Gladys was at work, but he often forgot or had a hard time finding Felix. Was he inside or outside? And then he remembered as you followed the surface curve of a Klein bottle in the fourth dimension the inside was the outside and the outside was the inside, making the location of Felix a mathematical uncertainty, maybe even an impossibility.

Hank

Hank Stone stood four feet six inches when he was in the eighth grade in 1963—a full foot shorter than his younger brother whom he called *El Jefe*. He did not begrudge his brother his superior height and the nickname was given with good will and accepted with equal good will. It stuck and the neighborhood kids, and even Gladys, now often called Samuel *El Jefe or The Chief.*

Hank was the shortest boy in his graduating class at Saint Mary Częstochowa Catholic School and the worst reader. His troubles led to what his family called his "nerves:" he sometimes broke out in hives, though since the doctor prescribed tranquilizers, he suffered less from the physical symptoms of his anxieties. But now his mother's plan was to send him to Morton East High School the following year. He saw trouble ahead.

Despite his stature, he had, with great deliberation, avoided intimidation and bullying thus far. The summer after seventh grade he started lifting weights. He set them out in the front yard in careful rows and lifted them there for several hours each day so everyone walking by could see how strong he was becoming. He led his small "gang"—five or six boys who appreciated his leadership skills—in a patrol around the neighborhood. Always cautious, but nonetheless quite fearless, he gained respect in his prescribed domain. But in high school, of course, he would not be able to rest on his neighborhood laurels. He did not have confidence he would be able to negotiate the tough guys, those out to make names for themselves, at Morton East.

He thought if he went to a Catholic high school—Saint Joe's in

Westchester, which at the time was an all-boys school—the discipline and academic rigor there (and possibly the lack of a need to impress young ladies)—would give him a better chance to survive. At thirteen, he told his mother he would be attending Saint Joe's and she helped him find an after-school job sweeping at the race track to save up money for high school tuition.

Hank had always taken his friends down in the basement of their house to hang out. His father's office was apart from the rest of the basement, and his father seldom left the office or bothered them. But by the time Hank entered Saint Joe's in 1964, his father had deserted the basement altogether. His Uncle Ladimer had come one day and taken out all the telephones. By this time, Hank fully realized his dad was—or had been—a bookie, a minor player in the infamous Cicero mob. Evidently, the same low status within the organization did not belong to Uncle Ladimer. He, by all accounts, counted himself a tough, an enforcer. The day that Ladimer took out the telephones, Hank overheard him talking to his mother, telling her that it had "cost" him to get his father out of the outfit without consequence, and that she still owed him money. Now she had to take care of "the sick fucker." He had told her, "Don't even think of divorce. No one gets a divorce here. You are not dumping him on me and Angela again. 'In sickness and in health.' Remember your wedding vows."

His father had moved upstairs and his mother moved Hank and Samuel down in the basement. They were elated to have their own unsupervised space, but a tiny, ragged hole in Hank's heart vexed him in unguarded, unexpected moments. Did the change mean his mother no longer cared what happened? She worked a lot, and the family no longer had meals together. When the boys went to the kitchen upstairs to find something to eat, they often opened bare cupboards and a refrigerator with pathetic leftovers.

One night around midnight, walking home from Bonnie Dempster's house where he sometimes managed to get himself invited to a meal, Hank saw his litttle brother Felix coming toward him in his pajamas.

"Where are you going, Bugs?" Hank asked.

"I'm looking for someone to take care of me," Felix said.

"Oh, Buddy. Oh, Buddy," Hank said, the words choking in his throat, his arm enclircling his litter brother's shoulder, turning him around toward home. "I'll take care of you." He was resoled to do so. It did not seem impossible at that moment. But,in the end, it would be too hard. He would fail to save his brother each time he was called upon to save him, and he would be called to do so again and again. Years later, when he stood next to frlix's body in a morgue, he would say to himself and to his dead kin, "I know somehow this is partly my fault."

A week after he found little Felix wandering the streets of the neighborhood, Hank passed out in history class. He suddenly felt very faint and fell from his desk to the floor. One of his classmates thought he was having a fit and tried to grab his tongue. The classmate's clumsy "rescue" roused Hank who bit the boy's intruding fingers so hard they bled. The teacher, who was oblivious to the context of what was happening and who responded only when she heard a scream and saw the blood, sent Hank to the principal. Fortunately, the principal, who had a reputation for strict discipline, was able to discern the problem after listening to Hank's story. "Are you hungry?" he asked.

"Yes, Father."

"When is the last time you had a meal?"

"I think the night before last, Father."

"Well, I am going to give you some free lunch passes. You can eat here in the cafeteria for the next week." Then he opened one of his desk drawers and handed Hank a candy bar along with the lunch passes.

"Thank you, Father." He replied mechanically. Then added with a note of sincerity, "I really appreciate it."

Because he had trouble reading, Hank was not considered a good student in high school. However, Father John, the principal, suspected he had potential. The principal himself had been a halting reader and had a soft spot for students who had the same difficulty. The concept of dyslexia had not yet made its way into the popular pedagogy of the day. Father John had noted how Hank excelled at mathematics, and so when Hank's chemistry teacher, Brother Avelino, suspected that Hank was getting good grades in chemistry class by cheating, and confided his suspicion to Father John, Father John defended Hank, telling the teacher to give Hank the next test alone in the principal's office to see how he did. Hank aced the test. The chemistry teacher shook his head. "Still, I think something is amiss."

In reality Hank was cheating on multiple-choice tests, but only in the sense of having devised a way to transmit answers to several other students who were doing poorly. He would rest the back of his head on his left hand as he worked, and then lift a certain number of fingers that corresponded to the correct answer of a specific question that he also signaled with his fingers. His co-conspirators sitting behind him discreetly waited to be signaled an answer, but followed Hank's clever advice to purposefully get a few wrong, so they did not all end up with the same grade.

Years later, Hank ran into Brother Avelino at the auto-body shop where Hank worked. "I really did understand chemistry," he told him. And then he explained the whole sting that he had designed. Brother Avelino had to admit he had been outwitted. Outside of math, Hank seldom got enough credit for his intelligence, and so he felt a certain vindication letting Brother Avelino know that he, as the teacher, had sorely underestimated his problematic student, and Hank also felt satisfaction for finally getting credit for the ingenious sting.

*

One day after school his sophomore year of high school, as Hank was sweeping the high stands at the racetrack, he was surprised to see his mother down below beckoning him.

"We have to bail *Jefe* out," she called as he came bounding down the bleachers.

"What happened to him?"

"He and his friends were shooting the gun near the Eisenhower Expressway. They got arrested."

Gladys had managed, with borrowed money, to get each of her sons a special gift for Christmas that year. Felix got a new bicycle. Hank got a microscope. And Samuel got a Marlin "Gold Crown" single shot .22. He had begged for it, and although she told him she did not like the idea of her thirteen-year old owning a gun, she acceded. Hank could see that she was allowing guilt for her neglect to get the better of her judgment. Now Samuel was in serious trouble again.

Hank sulked, thinking about how his mother had told him when he was a little kid that he had better never get in trouble with the police—that she would never be able to bail him out. Now here he was, an adolescent, taking up a collection for his brother's bail, trying to appease his desperate mother who evidently cared more about Samuel for whom she was bending the rules than she did about him. Hadn't *El Jefe* already taken his free pass when he played the Inquisitor and Uncle Ladimer rescued him from the police? But Hank quickly shook off the resentment. He took off his baseball cap and made the rounds asking other sweepers and even the stable hands to make a donation for his brother.

It turned out that *Jefe* and his followers had only wanted to get some target practice in. Along the expressway, north of Cicero, stood high and expansive embankments filled with bushes and trees and tall grass. They had ridden their bikes up toward the expressway and then bushwhacked their way through the brush of the embankment, taking turns aiming and shooting. Before long, troopers got reports of gunshots along the expressway and a SWAT team quickly was dispatched to surround the boys, striking them with holy terror. The boys lined up in a sorry row with their hands in the air, their faces pale with fear, two or three of them crying, one wetting his pants. They then were marched off to jail.

The boys sat there for hours. By the time Gladys and Hank arrived with bail, the troopers, realizing that nothing of consequence had been intended by nor had resulted from the shenanigans, and seeing that they had sufficiently chastised the boys, had already sent them home with severe warnings and haunting images of what could have happened—but without the new .22. Gladys told Hank, "I guess I narrowly escaped another catastrophe, but I still feel doom is around the corner." Samuel busied himself away from Hank in the basement, sheepish and guilty for having caused so much trouble again and miffed that he had lost his Christmas present.

*

Hank took pride in avoiding the trouble that *El Jefe* always found himself in. Hank had a more cautious nature and although he never ran away from trouble, he had the good sense to detect it ahead of time and not to court it. However, he had learned the power of randomness early in his life, when in first grade he stopped believing in God. He knew enough about his neighborhood and the universe to acknowledge that his turn for trouble would come.

Several months after he helped rescue Samuel, Hank and about five of his friends were playing poker in the basement when they heard shattering glass. A baseball bat had struck the basement windows, one

after the other and broken them. Jimmy O., Theo, Tom-Tom, and Arty
ran for cover while Hank lifted himself up to peer out one of the broken windows, assessing the situation. At this time, in the mid-1960s,
Hank's Hawthorne neighborhood was falling victim to more and more
gang violence.

The Ridgeway Lords, a Mexican gang from nearby Chicago's Little
Village, traveled through the neighborhood on their way to intimidate
the Arch Dukes, a Cicero gang from the Grant Works area. Such gang
activity proved to be more disturbing to the neighborhood than the
violence of the organized outfit whose rules and consequences could be
predicted. Because Hank's gang walked the streets of the neighborhood
without knives or guns and without organized protection, they turned
out to be an easy target for intimidation and sometimes were drawn
into scuffles. Several members of the Ridgeway Lords heard about
Hank and Samuel's basement hangout and that evening just after dark,
encroached upon what they considered an easy mark, knowing their
vandalism and bravado would make a strong statement about their
right to cruise the neighborhood. As he spied through the window,
Hank saw five toughs, one of which held a baseball bat.

"I'm going out," Hank told his friends as he grabbed a golf club
from a bag in the corner. "Jimmy O., I want you to watch from the
window. "Theo, when Jimmy O. tells you I am coming back, you open
the door and let me in. Then slam it shut."

As Hank spoke, he saw the stone white faces of his friends, frozen
in place. He did not think he could count on them at all. Yet, he felt
determined to confront these rivals who had disrespected his house. It
was a matter of honor. He went out swinging the golf club like a crazy
man.

"Maybe you guys will kill me," he said. "But a few of you'll be badly
injured as it goes down." He started turning around in circles with the
golf club stretched out whirling in front of him, ready to strike who-

ever might approach him. For almost a full minute, his erratic, daring behavior kept them at bay, but then the one who held the bat swung it, swiping Hank on the head. After a few random return strikes with his golf club, Hank fell to the ground, and the Ridgeway Lords pounced on him. One pulled out a knife. When the attack was over, they left Hank for dead with a wild whoop and roar.

Neighbors had been calling the police who did not respond until one neighbor swore to Jesus, Mary, and Joseph that the cops would find only a dead body.   Then sirens sounded and Hank, who in fact was not dead, was rushed to the hospital where doctors stitched him back together and iced his head to relieve the swelling and kept him there for almost three weeks. About twenty-five years later, when Hank suffered unbearable headaches and was then diagnosed with a brain tumor, he remembered the night that the Chicago gang had almost killed him and reheard the crack of the bat—a signal and an origin and one way to explain whatever went wrong in his life.

The rough and tumble of life in that neighborhood, and how did any of them get through it? (The short answer: many did not). Hank graduated from St. Joe's that spring. He stood five feet, eight inches tall (the same height as his father and his mother), having grown one foot and two inches, his full adult height, the last couple years of high school. A war was being fought in Vietnam (Jimmy O had enlisted right out of high school); civil-rights protestors had marched through Cicero, demanding fair housing laws.

Hank was looking for a better job and trying to cajole his mother to keep her from taking her own life.

Gladys and Hank

When Gladys swallowed the pills, she did not think, "I am killing myself," but rather, "I will be able to sleep." Likewise, when she left them, perhaps she did not think, "I am deserting my children," but rather, "I need a vacation." Hank was the one who had found her slumped over on the couch. He took her to the hospital where they pumped her stomach. This happened twice.

When she came back home each time, Chester started abusing her verbally calling her "slut," "cunt," "bitch." Hank put his hands around his father's neck and lifted him up the wall, slowly choking him. He might have killed him had not Samuel pulled him away. Chaos whirled around the family and around their once substantial home whose swimming pool now never got drained and was cracked and leaking with dead fish floating atop the murky water that was left, and whose taxes never got paid, and whose basement windows, shattered by the Ridgeway Lords, were boarded up.

Gladys sometimes borrowed money from Hank who had found a good job at Sears in its headquarters on the West side of Chicago or even from Samuel who was still in high school but worked after school at a hot dog stand. She borrowed from her sons, hoping to avoid having to borrow from Ladimer, but she did borrow from him too sometimes. She was trying to pay some of the bills. She was trying to stock the empty shelves in their kitchen. Her hours had been cut back due to her absence during hospital stays.

She worried when Hank's eye whites turned yellow. Was he drinking too much? His boss sent him to a doctor and the doctor sent him to a psychologist with a bad case of "nerves." Hank confessed his girlfriend had left him and it was eating at him. The girl had been Jimmy O's beautiful high school sweetheart. But Jimmy O. was in Vietnam now (Gladys had told him when he left, "We will save a chair for you"), and beautiful Rosie had many opportunities to sow her wild oats. For her, Hank had only been one of many in a row. But Hank had never felt so serious about a girl before.

Only years later, and no thanks to any psychologist, he realized that maybe he would have been better able to see the situation with Rosie clearly and sustain the breakup better if his mother had not been suicidal and if his father had not been crazy. Hank's bad cases of "nerves," which had been an issue throughout his childhood, could not be blamed on Rosie's inconstancy, her kind but wayward heart.

Gladys' suggested he take a vacation to Florida, and so his final "cure" for the breakup was to plan a trip to Fort Lauderdale during spring break. He had heard about the wild times college students had in Florida, and although he was not in college, he saw no reason why he could not join in the festivities with two of his friends. He told his mother his plans, and a few days later, she asked if she could have a ride down to Florida with him; he could drop her off at the Gulfstream Race Track, which was on the way to Fort Lauderdale, and then pick her up at the end of the week. She would help pay for gas. Hank knew his buddies would be glad for the extra cash, and that they enjoyed his mother's personality. Sometimes she could be a lot of fun (she enjoyed sharing stories, jokes, songs), and she had credibility among the teenagers in the neighborhood for having given Hank and Samuel full reign of the basement. So, he said, Yes, he would give her a ride and would not mention her departure to the rest of the family. Gladys did not really have to warn him that his father was not to know.

It didn't dawn on him at the time that his mother was leaving the family. She did not bring an inordinate amount of luggage. Her mood had seemed almost jubilant on the trip down. However, when he went to pick Gladys up after his week of beach parties and beach romances, she did not show up at the appointed time and place. Tired of waiting, his two friends hitchhiked back to Cicero.

Hank stayed over a couple of nights, sleeping in the car across from the racetrack entrance, the pick-up place agreed upon, hoping that she would appear, but she never did, and he never reported her missing to the police. Although in a state of agitation, leading to futile, dead-end searches, he never even once suspected foul play: no one had kidnapped her nor murdered her; he knew, somehow he knew in his gut, in the depth of the ragged hole that tore his heart, in the ache from the thorn that had made that hole, that she had left them—had left him. After three days, he drove back to Cicero alone.

*

At the Hawthorne racetrack in Cicero rumors spread rapidly when Gladys did not return from her vacation. Visiting old friends who still swept the stands at Hawthorne, Hank heard some of the rumors. Some said that she had had a long-standing habit of visiting the housing where itinerant groomers and stable hands lived, among whom were the only men of color counted on the Cicero census. Maybe she had fallen in love with one of them, leaving forever to follow him on his seasonal circuit. Others noted that soon after Gladys disappeared, her old boss Jack Viani sold his tavern and retired to Florida. Some censored her for deserting her children, the youngest of whom was only twelve years old, but others defended her saying that her current boss should not have cut back her hours just because she had missed some work while she recovered in the hospital; others argued she had no way out of an impossible home situation: she was only trying to survive. A few suggested that maybe she had not planned to leave at all, but once

free from family pressures, she just could not find the wherewithal to
return to the turbulence of her life at home. A few pitied her: alone in a
strange place, a middle-aged woman, childless, jobless, homeless. How
would she be able to start over? Soon the gossip subsided.

Meanwhile a letter from Florida appeared one day in the upstairs
mailbox, addressed to Marisol. A few dollars tucked in with instruc-
tions to buy some treats for Felix. A request for a few items of clothes
and a silver ring to be confiscated secretively from Gladys' dresser when
Chester was asleep, the clothes to be sent to an address in Davie, Florida, the ring a gift for Marisol: no words of explanation, only a request
to promise secrecy.

A few weeks after Hank's return from Florida, Felix, celebrating
his twelfth birthday, told Hank that his mom had called that day to
wish him a Happy Birthday. But Hank did not know for sure whether
Felix was telling the truth or only thinking wishfully. Later that same
day, Samuel asked, "Where's Ma? Has anybody seen her?" But Hank,
remembering his mother's secretiveness about the trip, adhered to his
sense of honor and said nothing. Years later, Gladys's three sons would
remember that time as a turning point and a touch stone and a deep
division: the time before their mother left and the time after, but the
three brothers never found a way to talk about it to one another.

Part Two: After
(1968 – 1995)

When Gladys first left, Felix kept waiting for her to come back home. He could not remember exactly at what time he stopped waiting, when he knew she would never return and tried to banish her from his mind.

Chester

Gladys's departure brought a spell of sudden clarity. Chester sat down at the kitchen table and started an accounting in a black ledger. Once, years before, he had passed the CPA exam. However, simpler skills would have sufficed to figure their financial ruin. What next? *How now, brown cow?* as the saying went. He would have to sell the house. He needed a job. Maybe some of Gladys's clothes and jewelry could be sold on consignment or pawned—likewise, his .38 revolver. He would recruit Samuel to help him. Hank, he could not count on. Hank hated him. Hank, he suspected, knew something about Gladys's disappearance, but Chester did not want to get Ladimer involved, so he kept his suspicions to himself.

Ladimer had warned him long ago, "Don't marry her. She's too independent. When push comes to shove, she won't stand by us." What kind of woman tries to kill herself? What kind of woman leaves a sick husband in need to fend for himself? What kind of woman deserts her children? He asked these questions, as though they queried novel experience, an unthinkable surprise, even though he himself had been deserted as a child and had known the drama and shock of a parent who courted suicide. Chester would be the one to get rid of her clothes, to clean the closets out, to pack boxes, and carry them out to Glady's old car. He dashed about with purpose and unbounded energy. Numbers in the ledger, on the calendar, and on the clock stood steady for the time being, but time, he knew instinctively, was not on his side. The numbers soon might waver or slip away. They might speak to him or repeat themselves or form a disturbing pattern on a grid. And then what? And now what? How would they proceed? *How now? How now? How now?*

He must act now in lucidity and with dispatch. He still knew people, didn't he? Those who could spread the word about the sale of his house; those who had accounting books he might be able to keep up to date as a job for ready cash or those who might know someone else who had such books that needed tending and those who could help him find a decent place to rent for not much money.

Samuel drove him around in Gladys' old Ford Fairlane, which Samuel, who had just turned 16, appropriated. Years ago, Chester's license was taken away for driving erratically and under the influence of alcohol. He no longer drove or owned a car. As Samuel drove, Chester ranted and waved his hands:

How now? "We will clean the place out, see," Chester began. "We will do the best we can. There's no way we can make it perfect. We don't have the cash to fix the pool or windows. Still it is a good house. Just not an eye catcher right now, so we will not get as much money as we might have at one time Do you think Flaminio might buy it? Then there are the taxes. All the back taxes." Chester clicked his tongue in dismay.

Samuel had never been privy to such talk before in his life. "But you've got a job now, right? We will be okay, won't we?"

Chester clicked his tongue again and shook his head, as though he had doubts. The numbers in the black ledger did not add up. His job was at a temporary service. "Felix still has a year to go at St. Mary's— there is that tuition. I guess it depends how much we get for the house. It depends what happens with that."

Samuel did not feel assured. He did feel a bit proud that his father was confiding in him, but at the same time the conversation planted a pit of growing anxiety in his gut.

Every night Chester sat at the kitchen table with the black ledger open before him, a bottle of whiskey next to him to swig from steadily.

How now, brown cow? How now, you ask? And I reply: Oh, I will spite my wife and never lie. I will teach my son to multiply. I will rob a bank as fortune goes. I will dance the night and stave off blows. I will keep the numbers in even rows. I will spite my wife and never lie. I will teach my son to multiply. I will keep the numbers in even rows, even as my fortune goes. And rows and blows and goes and rows. My wife, my son. My son, my son.

Hank was seldom around. Hank, when he did come home, walked past Chester as though he were not there. Hank seemed oblivious to the tumult around him, retreating to his room in the basement, smoking cigarettes, drinking beer, listening to Jethro Tull.

Felix wandered the neighborhood, disheveled and lost, sometimes brought home late at night by the police for setting off firecrackers, sometimes placated with a 100-dollar bill Chester might hand over to him on pay day to buy candy and toys, as though Chester had no financial worries in the world.

Within two months after they moved into a rented house in the Park Manor neighborhood of Cicero, a voice whispered to Chester that the words he spoke did not belong to him, that the numbers he wrote down in the ledger did not either.

How now, Brown Cow? the voice queried in a mocking tone. "The problem starts here," the voice said. "Discovery opens the way to more radical ignorance. All your words, all your calculations belong to someone else. Even your thoughts are not your own."

When Samuel brought him to the mental hospital in Elgin, he saw his father's file, which detailed his history as a paranoid schizophrenic. For the next six months, Chester was in and out of the hospital, picking up temporary jobs when his mind allowed him to think clearly. Then one day in winter, the police picked him up as he walked naked through the streets of the neighborhood, shouting to the sky one minute, crying uncontrollably the next. He was admitted to the mental hospital to stay permanently, leaving the three brothers alone, after yet another parental defection, that of their crazy father, to make their own ways in the world.

Samuel

Alone and adrift. Samuel had never felt so alone and so adrift before in his life. He saw the future unraveling before him with no one to help him rewind the ball of yarn; he saw his future spill before him, no one to help him gather the marbles that had fallen to the floor and were rolling away in every direction. Samuel was losing his marbles! One outrageous metaphor led to another. "Metaphors offer no remedy," Samuel thought. He needed a plan of action. He quit high school and got two more jobs in fast food, one at Burger King and one at Wendy's, in addition to his job at the hot dog stand. He and Hank agreed to split the rent and the bills, but when rent and bills were due, Hank was often nowhere to be found. He spent weeks away from home, shacked up with one girlfriend or another or taking refuge in a neighbor's home in the old neighborhood. Samuel paid the bills with resignation, as though he were finally paying the penance he had accumulated over the years for his sins: the sin of burning Anthony, the sin of shooting a gun near the expressway, the nebulous sin of worrying his mother, forcing her to leave forever.

Hank did come through at last. After his immediate supervisor at Sears Roebuck was fired for stealing, Hank secured his job purchasing for the sports department—he oversaw buying and testing possible new athletic merchandise and selected items to be photographed for the catalogue. He told Samuel he could help him get a job at Sears in the mailroom. He talked to a few of the women in the Personnel Department and calculated what needed to be done. He told Samuel that he would have to lie and say he had graduated from high school, but after doing that, the job was his and would offer him full-time work at decent pay.

Samuel poured his heart into the job and soon was transferred to a better one in the newly formed Information Technology Department. He learned about punch cards, which instructed the computer to organize data about sales and merchandise. He reliably punched the cards, for most a boring job, but for him a step on his way up (suddenly he trusted metaphors again: *the ladder, the corporate ladder*). He soon assumed the job of team leader on a line of punch card workers and was offered the opportunity to take a company course in FORTRAN and then one in COBOL computer languages. His mind matched the tasks set before him. Possibility loomed. But unfortunately, so did the military draft.

Those born in 1952, like Samuel, were coming up for the third military lottery. Hank, who was born in 1950, had survived the first lottery: his number, 264, virtually assured he would not be drafted. But when Samuel's number was drawn on August 5, 1971, it turned out to be an 8, which meant he probably would be called, and the possibility set him in a panic. He had just started to feel in control of his life again. He had his promising new job and not one, but two, might-be girlfriends. He did not want to go to war. He did not understand it. As much as he liked guns, he did not want to shoot anyone. He reluctantly went to Hank with a favor to ask.

"Look," he said. "Would you mind pretending that you are totally out of the picture with Felix? I think I might have a chance for a 3A deferment if I were to say he would have no one to care for him if I were drafted.

Hank shrugged his shoulders. "It's okay by me," he said. "I don't have to worry about the draft now."

Samuel had an idea to change the living situation so that he could make some extra money, and make it seem that Felix lived only with him. He considered Marisol, the beautiful girl who once lived with her father on the second floor of their old family home in Hawthorne, one of his might-be girlfriends. The years had added a vivacious friendliness to her other charms. Samuel and Marisol flirted whenever they ran into each other, and she had invited him to start attending Mass at St. Ignatius instead of St. Mary's in Cicero. She and her father had always attended St. Ignatius, not feeling welcome in the nearby Polish congregation of St. Mary Czestochowa. So Samuel, still a believer, started going to Mass at St. Ignatius, hoping to see more of her, and actually hoping also to see more of his other "might-be" girlfriend, Martha, who also attended St. Ignatius. He could not count anyone his girlfriend yet—Marisol seemed to like him, but she always kept their banter light and let him know she had plans to attend college in Texas. He did, however, feel comfortable asking for a favor.

Chester had ended up selling their old home to Marisol's father, Flaminio, who proved to be not only a good businessman, but a lucky gambler. It had been poker and horse racing money that enabled him to buy the house on 30th Street and later several apartment buildings. Samuel had noticed that one of the apartment buildings was for sale. His mind raced. If other people could buy on credit and make easy money, why couldn't he? Spurred by ambition beyond his years, he persuaded Marisol to ask her father if he might help Samuel find a way to buy it. Marisol promised that she would mention the idea to her father, but Samuel would have to "seal the deal."

Flaminio, Marisol's father, accepted Samuel's offer for the building, and not only due to Marisol's intervention. Flaminio had always liked Samuel's good manners and had noted his attendance at church. He thought Samuel might be a positive influence on his daughter who had an independent streak with wild ideas about Chicana pride and returning to Texas to fight for, for...he was not sure what. Flaminio even offered to carry the mortgage if Samuel could come up with 5,000 dollars for a down payment.

Samuel scrambled. Bank loans seemed out of the question. His applications were being rejected due to his young age and short history of work experience. If Hank had ever saved any of the money he was making, he would be able to help with a loan, but that was not the case. Samuel did not want Hank's help anyway. He preferred to write him off as a ne'er do good, always with a new girl, always carousing, drinking, smoking, off on an adventure, never going to Mass, never thinking about the future—leaving Samuel to pay the bills, to take care of Felix. Most of all, Samuel resented the way Hank always took credit for getting him the job at Sears. He wanted to cry out, "You got me a job sorting mail. I got the job in Information Technology." But Hank's pride at having been able to help seemed at the same time so strong and yet so fragile that even Samuel could not find the heart to shatter it.

Samuel had managed to save 1,000 dollars in the short time he had been working at Sears, but 1,000 dollars fell far short of what he needed. He confided in Martha, his other potential girlfriend who not only attended Mass at St. Ignatius, but also worked on his punch card line. Martha said that she had saved 500 dollars and would lend it to him if he would train to be a youth minister with her. Samuel was open to the idea and so welcomed the loan.

Then Hank came through again, though not with his own funds. Hank had befriended Dinosaur Dino, a disabled guy in the new neighborhood who was mentally slow but had a gift for fixing bicycles. On the street, he was called Dinosaur Dino because he had unusually long arms that swung as he walked, conforming to the stereotype of a cave man depicted in the cartoon series "The Flintstones," a cartoon that misleadingly showed dinosaurs living with *Homo sapiens.* Dinosaur Dino, who did not mind being called Dinosaur Dino, lived with his mother and saved all the money he earned fixing bicycles. Hank knew he always had cash, and so delicately negotiated a deal in which Samuel would pay seven percent interest for a $3,500 loan.

Samuel soon got the building and his 3-A deferment, and with this military and public acknowledgment, he began to truly believe that he was raising Felix by himself, in addition to excelling at work, running an apartment building, and leading, with his girlfriend Martha, a youth ministry. He was like Superman, the hero he had watched on television as a child: a man made from steel. And the building became his foundation on which to build a normal life, to provide stability for a future family, to reject his parents' failings, to become somebody respected and respectable. He would build from this building. Metaphors again crowded his brain, but this time helpfully. He took back his previous negative assessment: metaphor did, after all, offer a remedy, as did commitment to the heroic slogan recited on the television show: *truth, justice, the American way...*

Well, maybe getting out of the draft was not the American way, but nevertheless, he was reshaping his story from the one who had sinned to the brother (and future husband and father) who could excel and save others. Meanwhile, his hard work and busy life chased away any remnants of his bothering conscience or personal failings or doubt about the accuracy of the autobiography he had just invented. He lived a life of contradictions: of outwardly model behavior and of inwardly unending penance. He sometimes folded his hands in prayer, fingers laced in fingers, and he would stare at them and ponder: which hand was clasping which?

Meanwhile, Samuel rented Hank one of his apartments, thus helping him out again (though Hank perceived he was helping Samuel out again) and although from time to time and without fanfare or recognition (or consistency), Hank would fix leaking faucets or change hallway light bulbs, Samuel took this contribution as due payment. Felix spent as much time in Hank's apartment as in Samuel's. Both older brothers claimed in their interior understandings of self to be taking care of Felix, who had, most decidedly, fallen through the cracks when his parents left, and whom, in fact, no one was really supervising and no one cared for nearly enough.

He was a cute kid with a wide grin who begged for more approval and attention than anyone in the whole wide world had the time or the inclination to give him.

Felix

As a young adolescent, Felix Stone liked loud noises and trouble. He liked to show off. He had been known to drop a firecracker in a mailbox and to run away as it exploded. He had been known to find a revolver and to take it up on a roof and shoot it in the air. He could exhale perfect rings of smoke and did so often enough, for he almost always had a stolen pack of Marlboros in his shirt pocket.

He and his friends Jerome and Sal hung out the summer after eighth grade in the railway switching yard, where trains whistled and screeched as they backed up, hooked up, or uncoupled in the process of loading and unloading cargo or switching tracks. The boys would often look for unlocked box cars, or pry open locked ones with a crowbar and steal from them if they found desirable and portable merchandise. They had quite a stash stored in lockers in the basement of Samuel's apartment building, a stash that Felix used to bargain down debt he owed on the street when his ducking in and out of storefronts or his detouring through alleys failed to elude a collector who had spotted him and took chase. With time the friends got a feel for how the yard worked, which cars would be moved where, which ones would be stored for a while unguarded, and what the loading schedules were. They usually explored under cover of dark to avoid detection, though even in the daylight they had free rein of the mostly deserted long-time storage areas.

Most recently, he and his friends found dozens of boxes of S&H green stamps, worth thousands of dollars, in a freight car in the storage area. They worked for hours at night, three nights in total, with the help of two others and a strong wheelbarrow, to transport the boxes to Samuel's basement. The day after they finished the transport, they looked through an S&H catalogue, assessing what rewards they might be able to acquire for the stamps: a colored television set, a hi-fi record player, a gold-plated water-resistant watch, a Gibson guitar were among the products they singled out. In order to redeem the stamps, they would first have to lick the gummed reverse side and paste them into a collector's book, each one of which held 1200 single stamps. The expensive items the boys wanted required anywhere from 50 to 150 books. They were quite sure they had enough stamps, but the redemption process would be quite labor intensive. First things first. First, they would have to get some collectors books, which were given out free at many stores.

Instead of splitting up and hitting several different stores to avoid suspicion, they thoughtlessly marched together to the nearby Piggly Wiggly supermarket and demanded 500 collector books. The clerk at the customer service desk sensed that something was amiss and called the manager who invited the boys to sit in his office supposedly to wait while he filled their request. But, in reality, he called the police who came to question the boys. Felix's explanation that his parents had *bequeathed* him their life-time savings of stamps when they died did not seem plausible. Felix was no stranger to the questioning officer, who held no animus against the cute kid for his endless pranks, but also held no confidence in his honesty. He asked to see what Felix had, meanwhile giving a call to the FBI which would be the agency in charge of interstate trafficking, at which time he learned that boxes of stamps had been reported missing from the railway yard.

Hank happened to be home when the police arrived with Felix to inspect the stamps in the basement. When the dozens of crates, clearly marked with the S&H logo were spotted, Felix's lame alibi fell completely apart. Both Felix and Hank were taken down to the station and locked up. The other boys were let go. Hank was livid. "You tell the fucking truth or I will kill you," he said, grabbing his brother by the shoulders and shaking him and then punching him. "I am not going to prison for you."

Felix's face cracked open in tears. The two brothers had had heated disputes in the past, but Hank had usually relented and resumed the role of protecting his little brother: "Who's gonna help him if I don't?" he would think. And in silent response, Felix, whose self-esteem never soared, thought, "Yea, I'm so stupid, you gotta look out for me." Hank listened and forgave and came up with bail or a scheme, if needed.

But from this day forward the stakes seemed higher and the dynamic between the two brothers changed. (Felix started behaving in ways to elicit a brutality that Hank usually held in check. Felix would egg and egg him on until Hank exploded, and then Felix would respond to Hank's eruption with violence of his own. The forceful physical contact between them then became a type of cyclical familial intimacy: perverted, guilt-inducing, and sad, but firmly binding them together.)

*

Perhaps the police had been secretly observing the two brothers in the cell. For whatever reason, they eventually let Hank go and then Hank bailed Felix out after he was assigned a court date. At the court hearing, the FBI dropped charges. They mistakenly determined and testified that the boys had found the stamps in the basement and had not stolen them. They thought that the many crates would have required the strength of two muscled adult males to lift and carry out of the rail yard to a car or truck and never considered the ingenuity of five motivated boys with a wheelbarrow under cover of dark and all the time in the world. They suspected someone else who lived in the apartment building was to blame. They had started an investigation of an ex-con heroin addict who lived in the apartment above Hank's. The legal charges against Felix were eventually dismissed, but the deeper fraternal shift persisted. Felix no longer was the cute kid who nervously bit his finger-nails, easy to forgive—someone his brothers would watch out for, their wry-smiling Felix Boy, their favored and beloved Saint Felix, their dar-ling Bugs —but rather was becoming a troubled and troubling adult.

"Here is where you and I differ," Hank once told him, pointing his finger to his head. "I know what is what. I think about consequences."

Felix then danced a dance and sang an improvised song for Hank, titled "I Think about Consequences."

I think about Consequences
And Consequences think about me
The two of us together are as happy as can be!

"What are you? Some kinda comedian? Some kinda Vaudeville act?" Hank said, waving his hand and walking away, knowing perhaps that he and his crazy brother were not always so different after all, knowing that he, Hank, did not always think about consequences himself as much as he claimed, but sometimes further tangled the knot his par-ents (and just life itself) had left him to ponder and unsnarl.

"Look at yourself in the mirror," Felix shouted after him. Hank had recently told him about a misadventure that proved Hank irresponsi-ble. He had bought a black hearse to use as an everyday car and had driven it up to Montana where his friend Jimmy O was stationed. Af-terward, he and two buddies crossed into Canada with only 10 dollars to their names. They canoed down a rushing ravine in a "borrowed" ca-noe without properly considering where it would dump them or how they would paddle their way back, jumping out just in time to save their lives before the water swirled into a drainage basin. Eventually, they worked their way home: baling hay, cleaning apartments, detailing cars. Following in his mother's footsteps, Hank had quit his comfortable and secure job at Sears Roebuck to look for work that offered him more flexibility, a more expansive sense of freedom.

In the end, the ways in which Hank and Felix really differed were with respect for the law and the truth. Hank had never forgot Gladys' admonition to obey the law and not end up needing bail. He told the truth, though his code of honor sometimes resulted in few or no words in response to implicating questions. Felix, on the other hand, often lied and stole, continually called on his brothers to post bail. Soon he was taking drugs. Pot, and cocaine, and opium offered a way to fill a hole in his heart with numbness and a false tranquility. Hank did not partake—beer and tobacco (along with prescribed valium) being his entheogens, his spirits.

And so, they continued: Bugs and Hank with *El Jefe* paying the mortgage, sometimes generously ignoring the rent Hank owed and sometimes asking him to pay up. Hank and Felix thought alike in at least one regard: *after all is said and done, we must stick together. We three brothers. All we have are one another. We need a brotherly bond, a pact.* But Samuel was slipping away, defecting, turning his focus and his hope for redemption upon his job and upon Martha to whom he soon would be engaged to marry.

Regarding their future sister-in-law, Hank and Felix waxed skeptical. Martha regarded them (when she regarded them at all) as a threat— undesirable and unreliable interferences. She had ever-expanding plans for Samuel.

Felix lay on the living-room floor in Hank's apartment with a package of cigarettes and a package of balloons (both stolen from a boxcar) next to him. He took a red balloon out and blew it up. Hank sank back into an easy chair, stretched out his legs in front of him, and watched his brother blow up and then tap the balloon with the lit tip of his cigarette. Pop! "Martha," Felix said. Then he did the same thing again with two other balloons: Pop! Pop!—and said the same damn thing twice over: *Martha, Martha.*

Martha

"Fall in love," is an interesting expression, the official youth minister, Brother Alex, explained to Martha and Samuel, who were his teen leaders and whom he was coaching for an upcoming presentation the two would give together.

"What do we do when we fall? We hurt ourselves. We do it suddenly and without thought or reflection. That is the message of warning that we want to impart to the young people who come to our meetings. We want to substitute 'walk' for 'fall.' We want to walk in love."

"When we walk in love, we have time to reflect," said Martha, forming her response to echo Brother Alex's words and win his approval. "It is something we do together. When we fall, we fall alone. When we walk, the Lord walks with us."

"There is intention when we walk. We walk with purpose. We fall by mistake," Samuel said only because he felt it was his turn to speak. In truth, he was confused about love, but he followed Martha's lead and listened to Brother Alex. His wayward home life had not prepared him, he felt, to speak with his own authority on commitment and marriage. He listened and deferred to others when certain subjects arose in conversation.

"The important thing," Brother Alex noted, "Is that we learn to love ourselves as a creature of God, and we learn to love God, before we think about marriage or even dating. Look at Adam. He was happy, single in the Garden of Eden. God was the one who suggested Adam needed Eve. Adam needed time alone with God before he could successfully have a relationship with Eve."

Martha allowed herself to follow his logic and thought to herself, "What about time alone for Eve?" However, she did not say anything to contradict Brother Alex, partly because she never challenged religious authority and partly because she herself did not want any more time alone. She wanted to marry Samuel. She wanted to start a family. She wanted Samuel to take care of her and her children and her mother. She tolerated theological debates and lessons only to engage Samuel. Being teen youth leaders was something she and Samuel did together, and Samuel deferred to her when they worked at church. More than truly wanting to be a teen leader, she wanted certainty with Samuel. He acknowledged her expertise and followed her lead at church, though his skills in the Information Technology department at their "real" jobs far surpassed hers.

"He's very polite," her mother had said, but Martha had detected a note of warning in the compliment.

"Don't you think he means it when he is polite?" Martha asked her mother.

"It doesn't matter if he is naturally polite or not," her mother, Zina, had said. "Courtesy is not a natural attribute anyway. If we act polite, if we practice and exercise politeness, we become polite. We become a better person."

"So, you like him?" Martha asked. Ever since her father died, she relied almost solely on the guidance of her mother—and Samuel must too, she thought. She was proud of her parents whose own parents had emigrated as "White Russians" around the time of the Russian Revolution, first to France and then Slovenia and then to the United States. White Russians were aristocrats, she knew, and she often found herself feeling superior to those around her because of it. Her parents no longer had family money when they arrived in the United States, but they had their pride. Samuel would be lucky to join such a family. He was a good worker and motivated to get ahead, and so she was lucky too.

His own mother and father had, evidently, been sorely lacking, though Samuel seldom spoke of them: evidence of his parents' failures were his two wild, carousing brothers. She often assured Samuel that he was unlike them. She had not found an ally in either brother. Her beauty and sweetness had not won them over. They regarded her with suspicion, and she could see that they did not value social convention and decency in the same way that Samuel did. She competed with them for Samuel's attention, just as she had once competed with Marisol whose intelligence and independence, whose sauciness and ambition she downplayed as distasteful, unfeminine, or even a disadvantage to the competition she imagined and devised. Fortunately, Marisol had left town well over a year ago. She only wished that Samuel's brothers would follow suit.

"Yes, but take your time with him. Be sure he makes commitments," her mother cautioned.

"I do," said Martha. "I will," said Martha. "He will," said Martha.

Brother Alex was not only coaching them for the presentation they would give but also for an announcement. Martha had confided in him that she and Samuel would soon declare their engagement. She wanted to make a public statement to their "flock" after the presentation, right before the participating teens broke up into small groups to discuss prepared questions, such as "How will I know when I am ready to date?" "Is there such a thing as a soul mate?" "Will virginity and modesty and purity help me stay on the path to true love?" Martha herself had never doubted virginity or modesty or purity. She was not tempted to do so. Following the nuances of her mother's advice, she had come to understand these virtues as practical leverage, not only a matter of spiritual commitment. She could convincingly discuss soul mates and true love in a youth group but had little use for such abstract concepts as she calculated her future.

As Martha looked at herself in the mirror, almost ready to leave

home to give the presentation, she found that she was more beautiful
than ever. With the help of a hair extension, her long blond hair fell
perfectly to her waist in a long braid. Her white dress with an em-
bossed pattern was modest but stylish, her makeup was subtle, offering
the glow of health. She walked into the living room and looked into
Samuel's eyes to find his pride and his approval. He, too, had never
found her more beautiful.

She would read her well-rehearsed speech before the wayward group
of teens, a speech about commitment and "the walk" of love. Samuel
would stand by her side, and when she paused, he would read the pas-
sages from scripture which she had chosen.
And so that evening, he read to the gathered group a passage from
Corinthians:

> Love is patient, love is kind. It does not envy, it does not boast, it is not
> proud. It is not rude, it is not self-seeking, it is not easily angered, it keeps
> no record of wrongs.

After reading, when he looked up from the sacred words jotted in his
notebook, Samuel's body tensed up. He was close enough to Martha to
feel tension from surprise jump from her body to his as well and to hear
her slight gasp. They had just seen Marisol walk into the meeting room.
She sat down in a back row. She held a baby in her arms.

Hank

Hank never knew about the *Jefe*'s first child, and he never met the children *Jefe* had in marriage until years after they were born. He was never invited to the home of Martha's mother in Chicago where the couple first stayed, and the few times he dropped by, Martha did not make him feel welcome—indeed, quite the opposite: she stared stiffly ahead as he talked to Samuel and waited for him to leave. *El Jefe* had stopped coming to Cicero, so Hank and Felix felt as though they had lost their brother.

When Samuel sold the apartment building shortly before he married, the two remaining brothers moved on: sometimes sharing an apartment together, or when their times together got contentious, not rooming together for a while. Either way, they could often be seen together, after work at taverns, sometimes on fishing trips, and sometimes at the racetrack.

Felix had finished high school before Samuel left, thanks in part to Hank's nagging and in part, to the financial stability Samuel provided. Felix got a job as a horse handler at the Hawthorne racetrack after high school. His job would sometimes send him down to Florida following the seasonal circuit, and Hank accompanied him if he could get time off or if he was between jobs. During one of those trips, Hank found himself once again loitering at the entrance of the Gulfstream racetrack. He spent a few hours searching for Gladys at the place he had left her many years before and where Felix was now working for a few days. But he made a half-hearted attempt, wandering through the stalls, peaking in eateries, and mindlessly climbing the bleachers. In his mind, he felt that she was no longer there. He figured she had probably moved on, maybe with a boyfriend, or maybe returning to relatives in South Dakota.

On trips to Montana, Hank would stop in South Dakota to see if any of the uncles had heard from her and one time he looked up her sister in Wisconsin, but these siblings all said No, they had heard nothing. They said they were as surprised as he that she had left without a trace. Hank had no choice but to accept their answers, yet a doubt lingered. Maybe they really knew something.

For years, he never woke up in the morning with a sense of well-being, but always with a sense that something was out of kilter—sometimes it would take him a few moments to figure out what was disturbing him—and then he would remember that his mother had disappeared; she was never coming back. "I would just like to have said goodbye," he thought. As the years passed, the figure of his mother loomed a mysterious stranger, not the mother he had known and depended on. The only way he could explain her persistent silence was to say to himself that she was too ashamed to face them. He himself knew the feeling, having sometimes avoided old girlfriends he knew he had let down.

*

Samuel had often silently criticized Hank for not treating women well, for jumping from one to another. However, Hank did not see things that way at all.   He would go long months alone, and then when he did meet someone he liked, he tried to keep the relationship going. Like Samuel, he too wanted to get married someday. And yet his restless spirit often got in the way. He worked days in auto-body shops, a job where he could more or less be his own boss with his own tools, where he could use a gift he had cultivated for straightening and shaping metal, where he used his problem-solving skills to fix parts rather than replace them, where he found a way to feel free, to take time off when he could afford it, where he could come and go and then maybe move on to another shop. On the spur of the moment, he would say Yes! to a fishing trip or back-packing expedition. He was off to Montana in his black hearse, or he was off impulsively to Canada, Wyoming, Kentucky, Arkansas, Texas. He roller-skated with his friend Theo and took scuba and glider lessons, he learned to parachute from an airplane, and through these adventures, he forgot about his mother's abandonment and his troubles with other women for a short while, chasing away heartache.

In Hank's mind, he was stuck in a doomed, repeating pattern with women. He would fall in love, he would think about marriage, then he would get a chance to go on an adventure and leave for a month or two, often forgetting to call to let his current girlfriend know where he was, how long he would be gone, how much he loved her. When he got back, the young woman would be dating or engaged to or even married to someone else. Not fully admitting or even seeing his role, he found no way to break the pattern. So, he drank a beer, he smoked a cigarette. He took Valium, prescribed for panic attacks. He sat on a bar stool at the Lucky Star in the evening, drinking beer. He sat on a counter stool at Donna's Café in the morning, drinking coffee and doing the daily crossword.

The crossword was a habit he acquired and a pastime he did well, in spite of his dyslexia (or maybe because of it, having always had to pay attention to letters rather than words), having been spurred on by an old girlfriend, a freshman in college, who had taunted him for his Cicero accent and vocabulary and lack of ambition. Being motivated to "show" her, prove her wrong, he extended his vocabulary and exceled at the tricks of puzzle-solving that she had boasted to know as a sign of her superiority over him. And so, sitting on one stool or another when he was not working or was not fishing or was not off to accept a dare, the years rolled by.

Then about the time he turned 40, he started to get terrible headaches. Dr. Ramirez thought they were migraines and gave him a prescription for a high dose of ibuprofen. She also told him to get his eyes checked.

"I have good news, and I have bad news," said the ophthalmologist Dr. Kremski, who unbeknown to Hank, sometimes amused and sometimes dismayed his colleagues for his brash and cynical conversations with patients. Outrageous stories about him abounded: one inappropriate remark outdoing the other.

"The good news is you do not need eyeglasses. The bad news is you have a brain tumor the size of an orange, a navel orange, and it will kill you if you do not get it operated on immediately." After pronouncing these words, the doctor walked out of the examining room, leaving Hank alone in the cold room to ponder his destiny.

Too shocked to leave for several minutes, Hank sat shaking, staring at the random letters on the eye chart. He finally walked out of the office in a daze. The words "navel orange" kept repeating themselves in his pounding head. His old grammar school friend, Bonnie Dempster, was a nurse now and worked in another office at the Loyola clinic where Hank had just had his eyes examined. She had married their classmate Theo with whom Hank roller-skated along with Bonnie and Theo's two little boys, one of whom, Richie, was Hank's godson. Hank walked over to her office and told her what the doctor told him. "He can't talk like that," Bonnie said, knowing Dr. Kremski's reputation, but still horrified anew by the ophthalmologist's bluntness.

"But he did."

"I'm going to call Dr. Ramirez," she said.

"I'm going to the bar to get drunk," Hank replied. "I've got no health insurance. There's no way I can afford an operation."

He drove, barely able to see the road ahead, his head still throbbing "navel orange, navel orange, navel orange." He had downed three beers when the payphone in the bar rang with a phone call for him from Dr. Ramirez.

"You shouldn't be drinking," she said.

"Are you kidding me? What's the difference? I'm a walking dead man."

"No, no. I'm making arrangements for an operation tonight at Cook County Hospital. I talked to Dr. Kremski. We think you have a meningioma."

"A what?"

"Meningioma. It's a brain tumor, but not inside your brain. It grows between your brain and skull. They're usually benign, but they can cause serious problems as they grow."

Bonnie came to the bar to drive him to Cook County. Everything was happening very fast. He hardly had time to be nervous. Bonnie telephoned Bugs to let him know. She then tried to call *Jefe,* but he and Martha had an unlisted number—Martha's idea to filter any calls that Marisol or the brothers might try to make. Bonnie told the operator that her phone call was an emergency. Could she, the telephone operator, please ask Samuel Stone if he would accept a call from Bonnie Lewendowski—er, make that Bonnie Dempster?

*

In this way *El Jefe* and Hank got back together after many years apart, and Hank, once he recovered from his emergency operation, eventually got to meet Samuel and Martha's five children. *El Jefe* was kind to him during his long recovery in the hospital, talked to his doctors, visited with him after work, and on the day of his release bought him a membership at Bally Total Fitness so he could rebuild his strength.

Martha felt less empathy, but she knew instinctively her limits of influence with Samuel. She knew when to push and when to hold back.

When he got out of the hospital, Hank started dropping by to play with the kids. Martha resented his sudden appearances, but the kids seemed to enjoy him, so she did not voice her disapproval.

He was sitting on the couch with the three middle kids huddled next to him as he followed color coding to show them how to play "Twinkle, Twinkle, Little Star" on Sophie's new xylophone. Suddenly Casper, laughing, snatched one of the mallets and tried to hit Hank on the head with it.

"Hey, Buddy, my head just got cut open. Careful!" Hank warned as he caught the mallet in midair, but Casper, enjoying the trick and the attention, grabbed the stick again and managed to whack Hank on the temple before Hank, instinctively, swatted him away with force. Casper cried out, and Martha came running with baby Sally in her arms. "You have to go," Martha screamed. "I don't want you here. You leave me and my children alone."

"You've never liked me," Hank told her. "I had you pegged the first time I met you. You tore *El Jefe* away from his brothers. Oh, and if you think you're such a great mother, why don't you teach your kid some respect for sick people?" Hank snarled as he walked out slamming the door.

"Martha's very protective of the children. We send them to Montessori school. We never hit them," *Jefe* told Hank when he called him that night as Martha hysterically insisted he do. "She doesn't want you visiting the house unannounced. She doesn't want you alone with the children."

"Yeah, yeah, yeah," Hank said. "The bitch was just waiting for an excuse to turn you against me again. And Oh, Brother, you're so pussy whipped and domesticated, you easily take the bait. I hope you and your duplicitous wife both rot in Hell"—*domesticated* and *duplicitous*

coming from crosswords and Scrabble games. And then Hank hung up
and did not talk to his brother *El Jefe* again for twenty-five years with
one exception, and that was when Bugs died, but that conversation,
too, ended in further alienation.

Marisol and Samuel

When Marisol walked into the youth meeting with her baby Caleb in her arms, she did not do so to claim Samuel as her own or to exact any vengeance against him. She wanted him to know the truth, to know the difference between truth and appearance; he had a hard time with that difference and his difficulty had caused her trouble and had hurt her. She wanted his acknowledgement. She owed that to herself and to her baby, whom she had decided would carry Samuel's surname, Stone—along with hers, Piedra, an echo and translation—Caleb Stone-Piedra. Caleb, the spy, the Hebrew scout in the Promised Land. Caleb Piedra-Stone, the stone in the shoe, the one who could make the walk of love a bit uncomfortable.

Marisol had nothing against religion, but she had never before attended a youth meeting at St. Ignatius. She had gone to Mass at St. Ignatius with her father. She had received her First Holy Communion and her Confirmation at St. Ignatius in Chicago and had baptized Caleb a Roman Catholic at Our Lady of Guadalupe in Houston where he was born. But religion did not have answers to every problem. She always considered the youth meetings at St. Ignatius to be juvenile. She did not have to learn when she was ready to date or to make love.

She did need to learn how to fight for her rights and to organize voters, to expose injustice, to wear a brown beret. And that was exactly what these youth meetings in Chicago did not teach, but that was exactly what she was learning and doing now in Houston with the MAYO movement. They called themselves Chicanas or Chicanos, and some like her father scorned the name, but those in the MAYO move-

ment found pride in the term and in their own vocabulary. They called
that part of the United States, which was once part of Mexico, Aztlan.
Aztlan was the Promised Land that she hoped her son Caleb would
someday scout and claim.

After seeing Marisol with her baby, Martha made the announcement about her engagement in a shaky voice and Samuel stood next
to her, visibly uneasy, his face red. Marisol came up to them afterward.

"I want to congratulate you," she said, "on your engagement to be
married. And I want to introduce my son Caleb. Samuel is his father."
Then she turned around with the baby in her arms and marched out
of the meeting hall.

Marisol's affair with Samuel had been brief but passionate, if somewhat secretive. Samuel sometimes attended the priest at Mass. Marisol
had overseen flowers and altar cloths. One Sunday after the last Mass,
she and Samuel had found themselves alone together in the vestry,
putting away holy accoutrements.

"Oh, excuse me," he had said, when he accidentally brushed against
her as he put away the chalice.

"That's quite all right, sir," she said playfully, purposely bumping
him with her hip and then kissing his cheek, a gesture that Samuel
responded to by pulling her to him for a real kiss.

So began their liaison, which continued for several months in the
vestry every Sunday after the last Mass, their bodies entangling and
coupling on the daybed, on the floor, in a chair, on a large table; their
kisses sweet and long-awaited; their hearty lust bestrewing all that was
sacred about them: vestments and vessels, cruets and crosses, ordos and
oils, the wine, the blood, the bread, the flesh: the body and blood of
the Lord. All the while, Marisol was acutely aware that Martha worked
at Sears Roebuck with Samuel and had her own designs on him, and
that Marisol herself had plans on soon leaving to visit, and maybe stay,
with relatives in the Houston area where she could work at an uncle's

factory to save money for college and where, with her activist cousins, she could learn more about the Chicano movement.

It had crossed her mind once to mention to Samuel the letter she had received from Gladys years before. But, in truth, Marisol and Samuel shared few verbal confidences. Fingers and lips, glances and dares sealed their promises and inexplicit revelations, and although Samuel's eyes once flickered a puzzled flash of recognition as they noticed a ring with a seven-point star on her finger, neither the letter nor the name of Gladys was ever mentioned. Perhaps he wrote the ring off as coincidence or misidentification in the midst of more passionate concerns.

Marisol had learned that she was pregnant shortly after arriving in Houston. She thought about abortion, but when she confided in her aunt and her aunt assured her of her support, she changed her mind. She knew it would be easier on her if she had the baby in Houston, away from her Chicago relatives and their questions and away from her father and his criticism and judgment and interference. The aunt, knowing the stigma of the time, raised the little boy as her own in public for appearance's sake, but encouraged Marisol to have her own maternal relationship with him in private; his surname Stone-Piedra was reduced to Piedra if anyone asked or needed to know. After the birth of her baby, Marisol had moved beyond the factory, started taking college courses, and worked for *Papel Chicano*, a newspaper edited by her cousin Jorge. She helped him research and write articles about the history of Chicano exploitation in Texas; she volunteered to register voters and attended political protests.

Marisol had returned to Chicago that weekend only to visit her father, to introduce him to Caleb for the first time (her father suspicious of, but thankful for, the fiction of "baby cousin"), and pick up more of her belongings to bring to Houston. She had meant to make a point of talking to Samuel while in town, to tell him about his son and her new life—perhaps work out some financial arrangement—but then she had heard about the youth meeting and rumors of the engagement announcement. A pang of jealousy surprised her. She had never wanted to marry Samuel, so why did she care that he was marrying Martha whose superior attitude amused Marisol, who found Martha's thinking conventional and attitude pretentious? She shouldn't care or bother to give their engagement another thought, but the lack of public acknowledgment of her own relationship with Samuel, their secrecy in the vestry, which never had bothered her before, suddenly irritated her. In the past, she had found their "secret tryst" convenient in some ways: a few of her Chicago relatives had prejudices of their own about "mixed" relationships, and she herself knew she was not ready for a romantic commitment, but was more interested at that moment in a political one. Now, however, her newly found indignation spurred her on to attend the youth meeting with her baby and to confront the "perfect" couple.

*

Samuel had never told Martha about his affair with Marisol. She had seemed jealous one time when she had seen him talking with Marisol before church. and never had anything kind to say about her. In the days following Marisol's "scene," Martha, humiliated and angry, lashed out. "That baby could be anybody's!" she wildly declared and then berated Samuel when he did not immediately back her up or express any outrage. She threatened to break off the engagement but did not. Samuel began to suspect that she and her mother, whom Martha always confided in liked the advantage of having him indebted: he would have to appease Martha to make things right.

Although he would spend much of his life appeasing Martha, when perfectly honest with himself, Samuel had to admit that his worst sin was not against Martha, or even Marisol, but against Caleb—he had caused a child to be born into the world without a proper father to guide and support him.

Still he did not pursue Marisol. He lost track of her and of Caleb. When he talked about his children, Caleb was not included. He had five children, not six. Madeline was his oldest, not Caleb. Five fair children shone from the many photographs the family posed for before a professional photographer, with the dark-skinned child missing, or perhaps hovering there invisibly, and maybe Gladys, too, there, hovering vaporously over his regal mother-in-law, who took center stage, ruling from a throne-like wheelchair.

Through the years, he would find recognition in being a reliable breadwinner and a supportive and faithful father and husband and son-in-law, a family man. At times he would even buy into that recognition, finding satisfaction in his public image, convincing himself that appearance was, or at least could transform reality, could ease his loss of Gladys and the secret shame her abandonment had caused him, could mitigate the harm he himself had once ignited with a long-reach lighter and a .22 gold crown rifle and moments of impulse, moments of poor judgment. However, in reflective moments of self-reckoning, he would judge himself more harshly.

His denial of Caleb was the second of the three worst things he had ever done in his life. The third would involve his brother Felix.

Felix

Felix was about to go on a fishing trip up to the flowage area in Wisconsin and he asked Hank if he would like to go along.

"Who's going?" Hank asked.

"Jerome Birdsong and Sal Tonelli."

"Those clowns? I think I'll pass this time," Hank replied. Felix was used to hearing "I'll pass" from his eldest brother lately. It had been less than a year since his brain operation, and Hank was not drinking very much and did not care to be around heavy drinkers or drug takers. Besides, Felix knew Hank did not trust Sal Tonelli. Hank had once dated Sal's sister Mae and had seen him pull a knife on his own brother Ralph. Asking Hank had been a mere formality. In a certain way, Felix was glad he would not be going. His absence would mean that Felix got to be the kingpin fisherman on the trip, the one who would know the most.

"Are you sure you'll be okay with those guys? Do you trust them, Bugs?"

"All good," Felix assured his brother.

*

Felix and his friends arrived at the Wigwam Tavern in Hurley, Wisconsin (not far from the Turtle-Flambeau flowage in Iron County where they would fish) at dusk, just in time to watch the nocturnal flying squirrels glide toward the trees hung with bird feeders. Major activities at the Wigwam Tavern, which not only had a bar but a taxidermy museum (with the largest musky ever caught in the flowage, stuffed and displayed), included drinking (of course), watching humming birds and chickadees at the feeders, messing with red squirrels by playing tricks to divert them or scare them away from the feeders, watching the flying squirrels at dusk fly fifty to sixty feet through the air, grabbing a shotgun to shoot any bait-box-raiding stray cat that might be spotted, and boasting about musky or walleye or bass caught that day or musky or walleye or bass *almost* caught that day, as well as trading tips on live bait, lures, successful techniques, and successful sites.

The three friends had a few rounds of beer and then made arrangements to secure a Wisconsin fishing license, to rent a boat and spend the night bunked in the back of the tavern. Early the next morning, they would set up camp on one of the islands on the lake and then begin fishing from the boat for walleye.

The time being late May, they fished fast and efficiently in shallow water, darting in and out of shoreline protrusions, relying less on the depth finder than they would have in the summer, and using tail baits and toppers with contrasting lures. Felix had learned to fish mostly second-hand from his older brothers who had learned from the uncles in South Dakota. Jerome and Sal were not as experienced as he was, but they were willing to listen to him, which made him feel good. He seldom, in his life with two older brothers, had felt like the expert, the one who could be counted on to know something. They caught six walleyes that were "keepers," larger than 12 inches, that first day. With such bounty, they decided to throw a few back in the lake and to stay and eat at the campsite that night. Jerome and Sal made a campfire and started panfrying the fish, while Felix walked along the shore of the island, past a marsh to a very sandy beach. Suddenly he came upon the lower jaw skeleton of a giant musky in the sand. He picked it up and brought it back to camp.

"I'd like to show this to the taxidermist at Wigwam before we leave," he said. "I think this came from a pretty impressive musky. I'd like to hear what the expert thinks." And so, on their fifth night they returned to Hurley to meet Guy LaPorte, the taxidermist who told Felix, "Yes, indeed, this jaw probably belonged to a musky at least seventy inches long, right up there with the largest ones ever caught. This was washed up this season or late last season, probably from a fish hit by a motorboat—muskies tend to tail motorboats. It's good to know this size fish is still around here. None this large have been caught in years. Congratulations on finding the jaw."

Felix beamed. All around, the week had been a good one for him. Maybe because of this, he was allowing himself to be a bit more reflective than usual. He had started to think about his mother, which he usually did not let himself do. When Gladys first left, he kept waiting for her to come back home. He could not remember exactly when he stopped waiting, when he knew she would never return and tried to banish her from his mind. Now he remembered the way she sometimes had rubbed his head and called him "Bugs." She had sometimes danced with him and had sung her plaintive songs and told her wistful stories.

The next day, as he fished with his friends, he refrained from his usual jokes and antics. Jerome would later remark that that day he was already far away, thinking of another place, maybe thinking of death. In fact, Felix was not thinking of death, but was yearning for his mother and finding the lake itself peaceful and maternal. He recalled how distraught his mother had been the day at his grandma's farm when he almost drowned in the pig trough. His uncle had saved him with CPR and the first image he saw when revived was the tear-stained face of Gladys who had taken him up in her arms. "I could never bear to lose you," she had told him.

*

This was their last full day on the lake, and they caught eight "keeper" fish, though they threw several back, since they had more than enough to eat. They would pack in the morning and head back home. That night after supper, they drank, and Felix, who had been drinking less than usual on this trip, did drink heavily both beer and whiskey. Sal passed around a joint. Around three in the morning, Sal and Jerome climbed into the tent to get a few hours' shut eye before the drive back, but Felix stayed up to have another beer, watch the fire go out and to see and hear the first signs of dawn.

As the sun spread a rosy glow over the water, and the lake again summoned, he heard the gulping early morning song of an American bittern (the "sun gazer," as the bird was sometimes called in folklore) coming from the marshy part of the island behind him. Without thinking too much about it, he put on some waders and rubber boots and grabbed his pole and walked out into the lake as though into comforting arms. He was not expecting the under-current to be quite so swift as it brushed against his legs. He was very drunk and so was easily knocked over once, then twice. As he struggled to get back up the third time, his head knocked hard against a rock. The sharp pain and thud triggered an image, sudden and brief, flashing across his consciousness: the long-ago gopher whose head Hank had knocked with a rock, causing the gopher to die and causing him, the child Felix, to cry inconsolably.

But now Felix did not cry. The scene was silent. One might only have heard the gurgling morning song of the bittern in the distance, if indeed one had been present to hear at all and might have seen (if indeed one had been present at all to see) a gopher scurrying away, escaping hurriedly, as though now separate from memory, liberated from Felix's mind, vanishing past his still body, away with the current, swiftly, swiftly, probably to be forgotten forever.

Hank

"What do I do?" Hank had asked Cash back in 1972 when he started working for him.

Cash showed him a Chevy with its left headlight broken and left front fender smashed in. He pointed to the damaged left side and then the intact right side. "You make that side look like that side," he said. That was the extent of Hank's formal training in auto body repair.

When Hank had first left his job at Sears, he had taken a few courses at the Junior College and looked for part-time work that would allow him more freedom than his work at Sears. Cash had just opened his first auto-body shop at Division and Cicero Avenue in Chicago and had just married Jeanette. They had high hopes of making a good go of it when they hired Hank to help them out.

Hank learned by trial and error and in the process got to know he had a special gift for straightening metal; he had a feel for the material and took pleasure in running his hand over a damaged area to assess where to pull, where to smooth, where to weld, where to heat to make malleable enough to shape, where to apply a thin layer of Bondo and where and when and how finely to sand. As he developed his techniques and accumulated his tools, he took pride in his handiwork as well as his problem-solving ability. He mildly scorned those who just replaced parts instead of fixing them. Oh, he could jury rig, duct tape things together or use a clothes hanger instead of a needed wire when circumstances dictated, but he knew the pleasures of perfectionism and preferred them.

That first body shop had had two dwellings up above separated by a patio roof. Cash and Jeanette lived in one, while Hank rented the other. The neighborhood was overrun by huge rats. One night, Hank and Cash loaded .22 rifles with special bullets that did not ricochet very much and began shooting the rats down below from the roof. The rats scurried, a hit and miss affair. Soon a squad car pulled up, and the two friends prepared for the worst. However, the cop, instead of admonishing them, agreed that the rats were out of control and were immune to the poison that the city had put out. The cop even came back twenty minutes later with more bullets that would ricochet even less.

Evidently, the amateur shooting angered the rats, who being somewhat intelligent, formed a patrol, which began ascending the stairs, panicking Hank. He began to shoot willy-nilly; splinters of wood from the stairs flew in every direction, but the rats kept coming. Hank ran into his apartment, slammed the door, and peeked through a small glass window in the door. Cash dropped his rifle and jumped up on the patio rail. Jeanette opened a window facing the patio, laughing like crazy. She aimed a small revolver that Cash usually kept in a dresser drawer. She got quite a few of the rats and sent the rest scuttling away.

Well, that was one of the often-told stories of that era. And there had been others that pointed to camaraderie and good times. But Hank soon tired of Cash's stinginess. In spite of being friends since the second grade when a nun had criticized Jerry (aka Cash) for always trying to trade for better sack lunches or cash in on another's misfortune, Cash was now always hustling Hank, trying to get him to take as small as cut as possible on jobs. When Hank got a chance, he moved on to another shop and then another. Soon he was working with Benny who painted cars and needed someone to fix them. However, during Hank's hospital stay recovering from emergency brain surgery, Benny replaced him and wouldn't take Hank back despite Hank's desperate need for a job. Benny said he worried the surgery might affect Hank's mental stability.

"Are you serious?" Hank couldn't believe Benny, whom he had

worked with for years, would do this to him.

"What can I do? I can't take any chances, Hank," Benny said. "I've got a business to run. What if you go off the deep end?"

"I've worked with so many hamster brains," Hank thought to himself, but he responded with a shoulder shrug, not allowing himself to think about it, afraid of his own fury.

So now he "slung Bondo" for Cash again. Cash had moved up in the world, operating a very profitable shop in the far west suburbs where Hank now found himself. Cash no longer worked very much, just collected and invested profits, while Jeanette ran the office. They lived in a newly built, oversized mansion in Oak Brook and had a pet potbelly pig.

*

Hank got the call at Cash's body shop telling him of his brother Felix's death. He was being asked to come to the Mercer Funeral Home, in Hurley, Wisconsin to identify the body. While still on the phone, he rummaged to find the pills in his jeans' pocket. He quickly swallowed two Valium as his heart and mind raced and the muscles in his throat constricted. When he hung up the phone, he turned to Jeanette.

"I have to leave. Bugs is dead."

Jeanette, who was having a bad day, and was impatient with Hank for not always being reliable—taking time off, coming in late, making up excuses—replied without thinking, or before even taking in the implications of what had just been communicated to her, or, perhaps, given Hank's matter-of-fact voice, not believing it. She said, "It's always something with you two."

Hank slammed the door hard behind him as he left the shop without replying and walked to his car with tears in his eyes. He sat in his old car with his head on the steering wheel, Jeanette's words reverber-

ating. He was not sure how to proceed. He knew the jalopy he was
driving would probably not make it up to northern Wisconsin. Then
Theo and Bonnie occurred to him. Ever since Bonnie had helped him
the day he found out about his brain tumor, he had been seeing them
and their kids more often. The couple had visited Hank in the hospital
after his operation, and since his recovery he had taken their two sons
roller-skating, swimming, and on hikes in the forest preserve. He drove
over to their house to see if Theo could drive with him, using Theo's
car. Theo was about to go to work when Hank arrived. "Listen, Buddy," Theo said. "I just can't miss work today, but Bonnie might be able
to do it. She worked last night but has a couple days off now. I'll go
upstairs to see if she's awake and ask her."

And so Hank drove Bonnie's car up to Iron County as Bonnie rode
along, trying to give what comfort she could when she was not dozing
off. Hank found driving calming, though he did down a few more
anxiety pills along the way. It was a long trip, seven or eight hours of
steady driving, so when they arrived at the Wigwam Tavern in Hurley,
it was dark. Bonnie and Hank went in to get something to eat and to
make arrangements for bunks to sleep in that night—they would go to
the coroner the first thing in the morning.

"I always liked your brother Felix," Bonnie told Hank. "He acted
goofy sometimes, and he drank too much, and I know he had addic-
tions, but I could tell he had a good heart. I'm so sorry for your loss.
I'm sorry to lose him too." Her kind words touched Hank, countering
Jeanette's stinging ones.

*

The next morning, as Hank stood next to his dead brother laid out on
a slab, he recognized an expression on his face that he had seen before.
Hank remembered one time he had been in on a practical joke at the

stables. The gist of the joke was that Bugs would think he had won a 200,000-dollar lottery. One of the hands, Joe-Joe, had sneaked a look at Felix's number selection when Felix bought a lottery ticket and selected the numbers at the 7-Eleven. He later asked Hank to take a look in Bugs's wallet when he got a chance to verify the numbers—just to make sure he got them right. The next day, as was his habit, Joe-Joe wrote the winning numbers on the blackboard hanging in the office, only instead of the real winning numbers, Bugs' selection was posted. Everyone there, including Hank who had been asked to come to see the fun, acted nonchalantly when Felix strolled into work a bit late and finally went over to check his numbers.

Hank cringed now as he remembered the scene. His brother's face had lit up as he came running out of the office, telling everybody the news and what gift he would buy for each of them. When Felix finally realized he had been "had," the light in his eyes went out, replaced by pure dejection, the look that appears just as one is about to break down in tears. A cruel joke, and Hank felt ashamed that he had been in on it. He now recognized on his dead brother's face that same disappointed look, and that triggered a flood of images: roly polies and spiders, pilfered S&H green stamps, the runaway child in pajamas, gopher tails held up like trophies, and the tails of colorful balloons floating in the air, Felix's wide grin beautiful enough to break hearts.

"Somehow, I know I'm partly responsible for this, Bugs. I should have come with you on this fishing trip," he silently told his dead brother.

Hank blamed himself, but he also irrationally blamed Jerome and Sal, especially Sal. He did not believe their story—how they had rolled out of the tent in the morning with hangovers and started packing their gear, assuming that Felix had wandered off and would soon reappear. After an hour or so when he had not turned up, they had started to seriously look for him—first on the island and then in the water.

They had found him in shallow water with heavy waders on, his pole next to him, the waves splashing against him, his head, slightly bloody, lying on a rock. Sal was crying when he told the story again in the coroner's office, but Hank's heart went cold. He stared at Sal and said, "My brother was too good a fisherman to die like that." Anger and hurt distorting his usual reasonable assessments, Hank vowed to himself that he would eventually get the truth out of Sal and Jerome. However, before he could further challenge them that day, the coroner spoke.

"We can arrange for cremation. Is that what you would like?" He then lowered his voice to make the final sensitive point, "The cost is eight hundred dollars."

"I don't have the money," Hank said. "I don't have the cash with me. Could you do it, and then I could pay you when I pick up the ashes?"

"We could do it that way, sure. We're so sorry that this happened."

When they got back to Bonnie's car Hank was visibly shaking, and so Bonnie offered to drive. As they drove back, Hank told Bonnie the story about the lottery ticket. He broke down and cried. Bonnie was unsure what to say. All the sorrow in that family—more than she could take in. She had a place in her heart for Hank, who in grammar school she considered her boyfriend. Once in high school they had made out on his bed in the basement, but as she got older, she looked for someone more stable with whom she could start a family. She had remained friends with Hank, and Theo had asked him to be his best man at their wedding; she had asked him to be godfather to her oldest son. She fondly remembered the christening.

Hank had been late that summer day, causing her at first to curse her choice of godfather, until he arrived with 500 dollars for "the kid," five 100-dollar bills that he slapped down on a picnic table. He had left home that day with a 10-dollar bill in his pocket and stopped at the Lucky Star bar in Cicero on the way to the christening. There he played a game of coin toss, double or nothing, for over an hour and ended up with what he was sure would be the best gift at the party. He had had all the guests and even the priest laughing as he told of his meandering journey to the christening.

*

Bonnie was a nurse now and should have known appropriate ways to offer sympathy. But she was tired, not having slept well on the bunk at the Wigwam the night before—and Hank had not slept at all. So what came to mind may not have been fitting but was obvious. She pulled into the Motel 6 parking lot without consulting him. "I need to take a nap," she said, turning off the car and putting her arm around his shoulder and drawing his body to her, a gesture of comfort and ambiguous permission. "Let's go," one or the other of them said with a note of resigned inevitability

They fell asleep in the double bed with a disturbing painting of Emmett Kelly's Weary Willie on the wall above them. They dozed for a couple of hours before they made love, and as they lay there afterward she said, "Listen, Hank, if you don't have eight hundred dollars for the ashes, I'm sure Theo would lend it to you."

"That's okay," Hank said, appreciatively running his hand down her arm. "*Jefe* has lots of money. Did I ever tell you that I'm the one that got him his first real job when I worked at Sears? Bugs was his brother too. He should pay it."

When they walked out into the parking lot, Hank headed for the driver's side of the car. As she got in on the passenger's side, Bonnie said, "This never happened. It was lovely and sweet, but it never happened, and it'll never happen again."

Hank nodded in serious agreement. His friendship with the family continued through the years, and for years he and Bonnie kept their pact. They almost kept it forever.

*

Jeanette was genuinely contrite when Hank returned to the body shop. "I'm so very sorry," she said. "When you told me Bugs died, it just did not sink in. I'm sorry for your loss. I'm sorry for what I said."

"No problem," Hank said, shrugging his shoulders. He had always liked Jeanette. She countered her husband's stinginess, argued for Hank to get a decent cut on each job. However, Hank never forgot her initial reaction to Bugs' death and held it on some level against her. But Hank felt another stronger resentment against his living brother—a bitterness that *El Jefe* had echoed Jeanette's thoughtless words, or something like them, when Hank called him later in the afternoon to let him know that Bugs was dead and that they would need to get his ashes.

Bonnie and Theo

"How did it go?" Theo asked Bonnie when she finally got home late that evening.

"I am exhausted. It was a nine-hour drive. Hank got really upset, and I wasn't sure what to do. Are the kids in bed? I need to get to bed. I have to work tomorrow."

"Aren't you going to eat anything?"

"We stopped at McDonald's on the way home." Bonnie kissed her husband on the cheek and walked up the stairs to check on the kids and take a shower. She slept well that night. Within a week, she recovered from the trip, and her routine resumed its normal tenor. She loved that normal tenor; she loved her husband and her kids and her tidy house. She and Theo had created this stability together. Though their working-class background had groomed them for blue-collar jobs, Bonnie was a nurse and Theo earned good money programming computers. Her interlude with Hank in Motel 6 faded and seemed an impossible happening, something she had dreamt up in one of those confusing, nonsensical dreams or nightmares that come occasionally to almost everyone: disturbing, hard to shake off, but ultimately dismissed as nonsense. Hank must have driven their afternoon in the motel from his mind too. When she next saw him, no awkwardness hovered or prevented them from resuming their old roles as friends, not even a glance of acknowledgement. He listened with interest to what Theo was telling him about a new skating routine, and when Theo left the room, Hank teased her about a dying plant (a perpetual problem).

"I am either going to quit growing them altogether or have a service come in to care for them, like they do at my nursing station," Bonnie exclaimed.

Hank found this idea hilarious. "A good thing you are better with patients than with plants," he said.

Bonnie's husband Theo had spent his childhood roller-skating the sidewalks of Cicero and, with his sister Laura, competing at the Fleet-Foot Roller Rink in Summit. Now he and Hank often took Theo's young sons to the same rink. And when Theo was busy with a computer project, Hank would offer to take them himself or take the kids for the day to hike or fish or play ball or drive around. Bonnie felt infinitely grateful for the help. Hank was becoming a part of their family.

One evening, a few months after Bonnie drove Hank to Wisconsin, Hank and Theo brought the boys to FleetFoot, so Theo could show off his new routine—a complicated moon walk and grapevine pattern. Goofing around, Theo suddenly fell and wailed with pain. As Hank helped him to his feet, Theo realized he had dislocated his shoulder. He could see that his sons were too tired to endure his needed trip to the emergency room, and Bonnie was working a swing shift, so was not at home to stay with the kids. Since his shoulder prevented him from driving, and he rejected out of hand the drama of an ambulance, he told Hank to drive them all home in Theo's car, the car they had come in together. After sending the boys to bed, Hank and Theo spent hours telling stories, while Theo drank brandy, trying to numb his pain. When Bonnie got home at midnight, she found the two buddies slumped over the kitchen table, a brandy bottle between them, her husband without a shirt, his shoulder inflamed and swollen. Bonnie used the Fares technique, having Theo lie on the floor while she grabbed his wrist and pulled his arm in various arcs of motion to pop his sore shoulder into place.

The three of them sat up for several more hours, applying ice packs to Theo's shoulder, the two men retelling Bonnie the stories they had just been sharing—the story of the mishap at the rink and then the long-ago story of the night the Ridgeway Lords came to Hank's basement. Bonnie had heard that story many times before, but she listened to this new humorous version with pleasure and easy laughter, Hank describing and imitating the fear on Theo's face, Theo recounting Hank's crazed determined swing of the golf club.

The camaraderie and good will that night of ice packs and stories secured a bond that already had been developing among the three of them. At this point, Hank had no family except his estranged brother Samuel, so this couple with their sons counted as his trusted family. That he and Bonnie had in an unusual moment jeopardized that trust seemed impossible and the memory of their afternoon in the motel waned.

Marisol

Caleb handed Marisol a colorful crayon drawing. Without having to ask, Marisol knew that the little boy in the drawing was Caleb and the tall man at his side, dressed in harlequin, was his father Samuel. Marisol thought about Samuel more than she really wanted to. She did not pine for him or hate him or regret her decision to leave her life in Chicago, but she, of course, lived with his child and saw on the child's face Samuel's resemblance and read into the child's gestures and preferences echoes of Samuel's gestures and preferences or notable departures from them.

Celia, Marisol's aunt, no longer pretended that she was Caleb's mother. Still, Celia continued to be helpful and reliable—cooking, babysitting, attending school events—while her niece took college courses, worked late at the newspaper, or volunteered for one cause or another. Marisol had established herself in the community as eccentric, but a fighter for justice and a champion for Latina causes, including domestic violence, so the need to offer explanations about a child without a father or to pretend to be "respectable" in a conventional sense seemed less important. Marisol had done favors for many neighbors and counted on their goodwill.

Aunt Celia shared some of her worries about Caleb with Marisol—his preferences of clothes colors, orange, pink, red, turquoise—were these colors a boy should like?—the reports from teachers that Caleb had problems reading, that he spent too much time alone practicing dance steps or manically fixing the forever broken pencil sharpener,

that he once was found trying on a little girl's bracelet and had ada-
mantly insisted that it was his own.

Marisol dismissed these concerns as trivial compared with the in-
justices in the world, though sometimes she worried her son did not
have the self-esteem and grit he might need to be a spy for Aztlan, her
long ago wish when she named him after a Biblical spy. She still hoped
he would follow in her footsteps and fall in love with great causes as
she had done when she read Rodolpho Acuña's *Occupied America* when
she was in high school and had been able to suddenly contextualize her
shame—lonely afternoons at the race track, the only child there watching her father walk and groom the horses and she being asked, Do you
speak English? Where is your mother? Why aren't you in school? And
then later lonely afternoons in the apartment after school on the steps
reading, overhearing neighborhood children, "She's pretty, but she's a
Mexican." "I heard her mother died swimming across a river." "I heard
her father cheats at cards."

Acuña's book had banished shame and boosted confidence. She assumed her proper role as an indignant native whose homeland had
been invaded, no longer an outsider but an insider with justifiable
grievances. In grammar school, a stance of haughty silence protected
her against the ignorance that surrounded her in Cicero. But armed
with Acuña's book, she emerged a poised and verbose crusader. She
still had her original copy of the book, underlined and dog eared. She
brought its vision not only to her studies but also to stuffing envelopes,
knocking on doors, marching in demonstrations, and sharing camaraderie with like-minded Chicanas or Chicanos or occasionally sharing
her bed with *un revolucionario* or *una revolucionaria*.

She no longer attended Mass, and she smiled when she remembered
that she had once been in charge of altar cloths at St. Ignatius, a duty
which in one way or another had led her to Samuel which then led to
the birth of Caleb.

When Caleb asked about his Papa, Marisol tried to be as honest and positive as she could be: his father Samuel had been smart and knew about computers, and he knew how to fish. He was kind, but, unfortunately, he had another family in Chicago and could not visit them. Before Caleb started school, Marisol did not deter him from drawing pictures of him and his imagined father together fishing, roller skating, fixing a computer, reading books, and even dancing together.

*

"Do you want me to tell you a story?" Marisol asked Caleb one night when he cried that he did not want to go to bed.

"Aunt Celia already told me one. About *La Llorana* who kidnapped little boys and little girls. She always tells it to scare me into doing whatever she wants."

Marisol knew the traditional story. *La Llorana* kidnapped children to make up for the ones of her own that she had killed in a jealous rage to revenge an unfaithful husband. *La Llorana* wandered alone along the Rio Grande and through the dark streets of border towns looking for children to nab.

"Does the story scare you?"

"I don't think *La Llorona* will ever find me," Caleb said, "because when you're not here, Aunt Celia takes care of me."

"So very right," Marisol said, and then Marisol sang in Spanish and in English to her son:

Dos besos llevo en el alma, Llorona,
que no se apartan de mí,
Dos besos llevo en el alma, Llorona,
que no se apartan de mí,
El último de mi madre, Llorona,

y el primero que te di.
El último de mi madre, Llorona,
y el primero que te di.

I carry two kisses in my soul, Llorona,
that will never leave me,
I carry two kisses in my soul, Llorona,
that will never leave me,
The last one from my mother, Llorona.

And with that Marisol kissed her small child as she took him up in her arms and carried him up to bed.

*

A bright sunny day in late February several years later, Marisol was scheduled to collect signatures in the Greater East End neighborhood of Houston with her newest companion and love interest, Carlos Jimenez, but he called her at the last minute to say he had the flu and could not meet her. Though it crossed her mind that he might have a hangover rather than the flu, Marisol did not mind doing the work alone. Her organization, La Raza, encouraged working in pairs, but she knew the streets of the neighborhood very well, and she had canvassed them alone before.

The warmth of the sun, the chatter of squirrels, boat-tailed grackles and mockingbirds energized her desire to knock on doors and evangelize. The purpose of the canvass was to encourage voters to support a Chicano candidate, running against Gene Green, in the 29th district Democratic Congressional primary. The 29th was a primarily Latino district, which, unfortunately, in Marisol's mind, had been represented by an Anglo, Gene Green, ever since the district was created in 1992. She was supporting the candidacy of Ben Reyes and hoped he would notice her leadership and hard work campaigning—and just maybe (her most ambitious dream) reward her with a position on his Washington staff.

She had been going door to door for over an hour and was walking up a stoop to ring another doorbell, when suddenly she felt a heavy hand on her left shoulder, grabbing her from behind, and felt what seemed to be the barrel of a gun jammed up against her right cheek and a deep voice asking for her purse. She knew so well the drill: Hand over your bag. Offer no resistance. And yet, she could not believe that the situation loomed beyond her control. She knew these cocky *pandilleros* very well. She could not simply let them have their way. She was a woman who firmly believed that her destiny and her future were always and everywhere in her own hands. She held full confidence that she could change the world.

Samuel

True, Samuel had money. He continued to climb the metaphoric ladder, the corporate ladder; headhunters had scouted his talent, made offers and he was now a director in the Information Technology department at Blue Cross. Each month, the company contributed to his pension. It provided the personal health coverage given to supervisors, which meant thorough annual check-ups and plenty of preventive medicine. He had stocks and bonds and annuities. He had life insurance and health insurance for his family and had four-week vacations when he could get away to take them. The company paid for college courses and for his deluxe health club membership. He had a good salary with annual raises. Indeed, Samuel had money, but he also had expenses.

His five children had been born in rapid succession: Madeline, Steven, Sophie, Casper, Sally: girl, boy, girl, boy, girl. Martha noted that they needed another boy to even the spread, but Samuel shook his head and vowed to himself to buy condoms to supplement Martha's chart of her cycle as he silently remembered a boy he already "had" who could easily "even the spread" by going to the head of the line, while also recollecting and recalculating the cost of tuition at Joliet Montessori. Martha was a true believer, not only in the Catholic rhythm method, but also in the Montessori method, and he usually followed her lead regarding family matters and methods. While she was more likely to consult with her mother than with him about the details of child-caring, he enjoyed the household bustle and commotion of family life with small children afoot and was always willing to do his part (change diapers, make supper, drive a child to an appointment) in exchange for the security circumscribed by Martha's maternal instincts and stay-at-home calling. Her commitment to family matched his, for the failures of his childhood family drove him to prove he could do much better, propelled him to succeed at home and at work, "to bring home the bread, the bacon, the bananas and bonanzas" via the long train commute to his family in Will County from the Chicago loop.

He did not question the sacrifices he made, the penance he could not stop himself from serving: fathering five children (though he had hoped to stop at two), withstanding the pressures of a high stakes job, taking extra courses at Lewis University to acquire the knowledge demands of said job—but, nevertheless, he always assumed Martha made more sacrifices than he. He seldom questioned her (and her mother's) demands, nor did he ever refuse Martha more money. But now Madeline and Steve were being fit for braces and now a bigger house would be needed in a safer community and now new shoes for fast-growing feet and now, according to his kids, all the kids in the world were getting barracuda boats and teacher-Barbies for Christmas and now enough money had to be set aside for college funds—but no, please no, not another baby, he thought as he lifted little Sally up in his arms with pure paternal joy.

Then the letter came from Houston.

Oh, yes, another wrench was needed to throw into the mix, just as it had been needed last year when Bonnie Dempster called about Hank and his brain operation, and so he, Samuel, had tried then to take care of that, and just when he had taken care of that, that is, just when Hank's hospital stay was over, and Samuel no longer had to rush to Cook County Hospital after work every night, yes, just then (or shortly after just then) came the scene Hank had caused with his wife over Casper and then its aftermath: the heated altercation on the phone between brothers. Well, he could and would have to put that out of his mind: there simply was no time to reflect, because he was late, late for a work meeting, late for a teacher conference, late to take

Martha's mother to the doctor, late to meet Martha to look at a new house with enough bedrooms and bathrooms for their large family in a safe and expensive neighborhood, late to change the car's oil, late for the computer class on JavaScript, late for Madelene's play, *Our Town*, and Sophie's choir concert, American folksongs with the New Lenox Singers, and late to meet up with an employee he supervised named Sunny whom he had been told to fire.

The letter explained that Marisol had been shot, killed. Samuel had not spoken to her since that night long ago at the Youth Meeting when she had told him he was the father of Caleb. It had been easy enough to follow Martha's lead and try to convince himself to question whether the child was his, or, even if his, easy to meld this mistake too into the penance for wrongdoing he daily tallied. Evidently, Marisol had been gathering signatures for an upcoming local election in a bad neighborhood when a gang member tried to rob her and ended up shooting her. She had died within an hour of being taken to the hospital. Her aunt, who had served as a caretaker to the boy since he was born, was now too old and sick to continue doing so alone. Caleb was staying with a cousin and the cousin was writing Samuel for financial help. He couldn't get the tune out of his mind, the folk song Sophie practiced every day for her concert: *Black Sheep, black sheep, where d'you leave your lamb? Way down in the valley.*

Well, Samuel would have to talk to this cousin in person to find out exactly what was what, and he probably would have to tell Martha. He saw no way he could avoid telling her or saw no way to lie to keep things on an even keel, but he dreaded her reaction. She had nearly broken off their engagement when she first found out about Caleb, but over the years the humiliation of the night at the Youth Meeting had receded.

"You should ask for a DNA test," she said coldly when he finally got up enough nerve to have the conversation. "You have the welfare of your own children to worry about."

However, when Samuel finally went to Houston to meet the cousin and saw the fourteen-year-old Caleb, he saw no need for a DNA test. Caleb was a slightly darker version of Samuel: the same overlapping tooth, the same flared nostrils and high cheekbones and square jaw and stare and gait—same, same, same, the same but slightly off—a dark caricature in loudly colored clothing, to taunt him. The resemblance was unnerving, but, at that moment, it did not open up Samuel's heart or stir his paternal instinct; on the contrary, it steeled his resolve to settle this matter expeditiously and with as little financial harm to his "real" family as possible. The implications of biology sent him reeling. Who was this child to him? Just because he had waltzed around a priest's dressing room once upon a time with the child's mother, he would not allow this child to threaten all that he had worked so hard to create. His "true" family dressed conservatively, had demure smiles on their faces, lived in a princely house and numbered seven, eight with his mother-in-law, and he had a whole trove of professional photographs to prove it.

Samuel remained calm as he spoke with the cousin, scrutinizing her words to assess the shrewdness behind them. He wrote her a check, a large check (but probably not nearly so large as he would have to write if she took him to court), but he feared, correctly, that the ordeal would come back again to haunt him—and, most annoyingly, the child was calling him Papa.

Samuel later told Martha, "I just don't see myself as the type of person who finds himself in a situation like this. I am not this type of person—and yet, here I am." He was staring at a family photograph on the bedroom wall, him in the middle, dressed in a suit, Martha next to him in a lovely dress, holding the back of a wheelchair in which sat her regal mother, and her and Samuel's progeny—fair and lovely girls and boys with photogenic smiles and poses—spread around them.

All the next week and for weeks after that, time and again, he found himself humming the haunting melody, the words barely remembered but tripping on his tongue and lips, the song from Sophie's concert that she had practiced at home: *My mother told me before she went away to take good care of the baby. But I went out to play and the baby ran away, and the poor little lamb cryin' Mama.*

*

Amid this turbulence, Hank called *Jefe* to tell him about Felix. Samuel balked: First, Hank should not be calling him at all without first apologizing for the way he had last spoken to him. Second, who were these brothers to him anymore anyhow anyway? Were they his brothers only to take him down with them into their spiral of ruin? *Drowned?*

Again, the obtuseness of biology befuddled him: "We had the same mother, yes, true enough—a woman who deserted us—so how does that tie me to them forever?" How many times had he bailed his brother Felix out of a jail when he lived with him in his apartment building? How many times had he paid Hank's share of the rent when they supposedly shared expenses? How many nights had he visited Hank in the hospital when he had his surgery? He had done enough for his brothers.

Love keeps no record of wrongs: he had once read these words aloud at a long-ago youth meeting. The passage came back to him, an unexpected jolt. He had never sorted out that tangled brotherly love. He had forsaken it, thinking he could start anew with another family, without residue from his first troubled family. Now his brother had drowned just when Samuel was drowning too in weedy entanglements within the family he had started.

"Just let it be," Samuel told Hank. "Just let it be. I can't get involved." And then he hung up the phone.

Many years later in the forest preserve where his brother Hank had often hiked, Samuel would have a frank reckoning about his brothers, both of whom would be dead by then. When he came to the part about Felix and his ashes, Samuel choked up with a singular mixture of sorrow, anger, guilt. "It was Hank's responsibility," he would say, almost in tears. But even as he lamely defended himself, he suddenly realized—delayed in his discernment—that his refusal to help and his refusal to mourn with his surviving brother Hank the loss of his dead brother Felix ranked among his most shameful deeds: right up there with leaving a baby son unclaimed or burning a martyr at the stake.

Part Three: And Then After That
(1995 – 2015)

Where their mother had died, or even where she had lived for the past 40 years was not relevant, was not the point.

Ruthie

As he tried to explain himself, her hand instinctively reached out to reassure him. An image flashed through her mind, a painting she had seen in Madrid at the Prado. *Noli me tangere* by Correggio. At the time, the painting had brought tears to her eyes. In it, Jesus had just risen from the dead. He had not had time yet to assimilate all that had happened to him, especially to his body. He was pointing toward Heaven as if to say to Mary Magdalene whose hand reached to comfort him, "Wait a minute. I have to find my bearings. I need to pray to my Father in Heaven before I can begin again. Please just don't touch me yet." All of this flashed through Ruthie's mind in a mere second. She drew her hand back. She had been assaulted once in a strange city and afterward her body too had been sensitive, as vulnerable as she sensed his to be. For a long time she had shunned being touched.

She had just met Hank, but his vulnerability and her recall of the painting drew her to him. So did his neighborhood accent and down-to-earth perceptions and unrestrained bursts of wonder and enthusiasm; he reminded her of the scruffy, unpretentious neighbor boys whom she had grown up with on the Southwest side of Chicago. The way he readily saw farfetched similarities between himself and her as amazing coincidences (surely portending lasting bonds) amused her and endeared him to her ("That's just like *me*! I do too!" he exclaimed, pointing to his chest with his index finger with genuine surprise). She had just mentioned how much she enjoyed riding along the lakefront on a bicycle. They kept talking and in the midst of their talk she impulsively reached out. Suddenly she was *falling* in love (*falling, falling,* not *walking* cautiously). She seldom fell in love, but when she did, it happened in an instant with great certainty.

Ruth Winters had traveled a lot: Rabat, Madrid, Istanbul, Heidelberg, Sowa, Kyoto, Cuernavaca, Lima. These are eight cities where she had taught English. Past the age of 40, she now was settling down in Chicago, the city where she had grown up. Growing up, not so cosmopolitan in outlook then, her paternal aunt, who had raised her after the death of her mother, seldom allowing her to leave their West Lawn neighborhood—until finally she escaped to college. And then the wide world had opened up and she had left her troubled childhood and her neighborhood far behind.

After finding a job, an apartment, she had spent her first summer back in the town riding the lakefront on a bicycle when she was not teaching English at an immigrant center or teaching drawing at the YWCA. Long bicycle rides as well as long walks cleared her mind. She had gone back to her old neighborhood only once to make an obligatory visit to her aunt and to her father who was now living in her aunt's house, their old childhood home and hers.

She was on a bicycle tour one Sunday morning in late May when she met Hank who had signed up for it, figuring he could learn a few things about the city. He had been coming downtown on his own to bicycle for months, building up strength after his brain operation and saving up questions about the buildings, the bridges, the tunnels, the parks. The tour highlighted buildings along north Lake Shore Drive visible from the bicycle path. He sidled up to her on his bicycle and they stopped and listened together to the guide explain the Mies apartment buildings at 800 North Lake Shore Drive. Then they rode slowly along together toward the next stop. "I'm kinda like that Mies guy when I work," Hank told her.

"How so?"

"I fix cars and I stare at a problem and think about it for a long time before I start working. Isn't that what the guy said Mies did? When I finally put my hands on the job, I know exactly what I need to do." Ludwig Mies van der Rohe, the guide had told them, sat in a folding chair for a month across the street from the site, staring at the empty site, before beginning his plans for the apartment buildings.

"There is a lot to be said for daydreaming," Ruthie assented. "I take long walks before I write or draw. I live a lot in my head, but one reason I like to look at the buildings is that they take me outside myself and force me to notice details, the material world."

They continued to talk after the tour, exchanging condensed life histories, ordering soft drinks in Grant Park, sitting at one of the outdoor tables in front of the drink stand. Ruthie noticed that he glanced down at her hands when she took off her cycling gloves as if to check out her ring finger. When she told him she had been teaching English overseas for years, Hank said humbly, "Not my best subject. I have dyslexia."

He said he'd ride back with her to Montrose Harbor where she had parked her pick-up truck. The ride glided along with the wind to their back, but Hank noted that his ride back would be difficult. "I hadn't thought about that," Ruthie said. "When things are easy for me, I don't always think ahead about the consequences," Ruthie said.

"Once I got in canoe and floated down a ravine. I didn't think how I would get back. I ended up almost drowning when the current rushed toward a basin," he laughed. Then one *drowning* led to another and he told her about the death of Felix. The story seemed to spill from his mouth, its aftermath casting a solemn intimacy over the rest of their ride. As Ruthie rode in silence thinking about the drowning, she thought she understood what had inspired the imagery that had flashed through her mind when she first met him: *Noli me tangere.*

When they got to Montrose, they walked out to the end of the pier to view from a distant perspective the downtown skyline they had just been a part of, pointing out to each other some of the buildings they had just learned about on their tour. "Let's meet downtown again next Sunday," he said. "And check out some more of the buildings."

"Yeah, okay, let's do that," she agreed.

"If you want, you can drive and park in front of the Picasso. Parking is free on Sundays. I usually get there by seven o'clock."

"Okay," she said. "I'll meet you there at seven."

When they parted, Ruthie realized they had not exchanged phone numbers or even last names. What if something happened, and he could not show up? Ruthie would have no way to get in touch with him. The prospect nagged at her all week: she very much wanted to see him again.

Samuel

Unlike most of his colleagues, Samuel enjoyed the corporate workshops that were annually required, especially those that focused on psychology and human relations. He applied what he learned not only at work, but also at home as he negotiated the morass of family dynamics. Like most parents, he wanted his children to have more opportunities than he had had and a more stable home life. However, he did not disparage his mother for her abandonment. He did not like to think or talk about his mother, but when he did think about her, he knew that he loved her and wanted to know how to forgive her. Although his wife could not countenance his past, he did not hold it against her; he was, in the end, grateful to Martha for being different from Gladys, for providing their children with full devotion and reliability.

At one of the corporate workshops he learned that *perception is reality*. He thought about what this meant a lot. He thought about it one day when his youngest daughter Sally complained that she was no longer a baby and needed to be allowed to go on a sleepover; he thought about it another day when his middle daughter Sophia also complained that she was no longer a child and was old enough to watch *Sex and the City*; he thought about it when his son Casper told him in all seriousness that he had not lied when he said he did not use his father's drill—he had fibbed, which was quite different, and evidently a much less grave offense. Samuel's openness and pensiveness and bemusement and distractions made him a rather permissive and approachable parent.

*

One summer Sunday morning Martha went to Mass with their children, but Samuel didn't accompany them. He feigned a headache and exhaustion from work, but instead of resting at home, he drove to Cicero. He parked his car near Woodbine Public School and sat on a bench shaded by oak trees in front of the school. From this concealed spot he could see his childhood home and other homes of his old neighborhood.

Cicero's population was changing. Mexican Americans from Back-of-the-Yards and Little Village neighborhoods in Chicago had bought up or were buying up most of the houses and real estate. When the Mexicans started moving in, panic, fueled by real estate interests, took hold, creating white flight. Most of those of Polish or Italian or Bohemian descent moved from the town, leaving the neighborhoods they had grown up in and had raised their children in, fearing crime or neighborhood deterioration or dropping housing prices or just acting upon ingrained or incited prejudice toward those with brown and black skin.

Actually, Samuel's old childhood house looked better now than it did when his father sold it to their upstairs tenant, Faminio, arguably even better than when they had lived there. The basement windows had been replaced, the swimming pool removed, the old siding restored. Beds of colorful flowers graced the freshly mowed lawn. He recalled that Gladys had once sprinkled four o'clock seeds in front of the house when they lived there, flowers that bloomed in late summer, and these her children had found beautiful, but for most of the growing season only grass and dandelions had grown in the yard.

This was not the first time that Samuel sat on the bench to gather his thoughts and wait. He had come several times before, finding time from his busy weekly schedule on Sunday mornings by skipping Mass with one plausible excuse or another. From time to time, gossip or bits of information about those in his old neighborhood filtered down to him from Wylie, an old friend who called him once every two years or so. In passing, Wylie had mentioned that Anthony Pietrowski still lived in the neighborhood. Evidently Anthony had inherited his parents' house, a house visible from where Samuel sat.

Samuel did not necessarily want to talk to Anthony. He just wanted to connect with what had started it all, what had started his path away from innocence, a path that had led him to forsake a son and a brother. He just wanted to observe Anthony again as he had observed him another Sunday morning as Anthony was walking back home from Mass at St. Mary of Czestochowa Catholic Church whose tall twin copper spires could be seen from almost any spot in the neighborhood and which stood majestically a few blocks away. That previous Sunday Anthony had been walking and talking with a boy of about ten. Perhaps he was married and had a child?

Perception is reality. Samuel knew that to be true. Samuel, ever respectful of expert opinion and public judgment, was not one to question the veracity of what had been taught in a sanctioned setting, nor the limits of its wisdom. He had learned the lesson in a professional class at work and practiced its message at home and on the job. And yet Samuel wondered if his need to adjust his own perception of childhood caused him to come to Cicero these Sunday mornings, or if he hoped to find some reassurance that others' perceptions did not encircle him in any lasting blame or frame him in ill repute. If he got a chance to meet up with Anthony, would they laugh togther at their childhood prank? Would any bad feelings linger?

Judging from the parade of people walking home from church, Mass now was over. Samuel did not see Anthony in the crowd this time, but he would come again and maybe talk to him These pilgrimages to his old neighborhood allowed him some precious time alone to think.

Samuel, sitting there inconspicuously on a bench on a sunny summer morning, pondered not only the nature of reality, but also the
nature of evil. How could evil exist and be defined by consequences
when intentions had only been thoughtless or wayward or maybe even
innocent? He turned this question over in his mind. He considered his
own behavior: the worst things he had ever done, the ones he regretted
and the ones that affected others: Anthony, Caleb, his brothers. And
being now so physically near his childhood home, he considered too
the behavior of those who had once lived there with him. He thought
about his father and brothers. And then he allowed himself to think of
his mother, Gladys. Did she ever find the time in a quiet place wher-
ever she might be to wonder about him, to think about what she had
done, about those she had left behind? *Black sheep, black sheep, where
d'you leave our lamb?*

It hurt viscerally to think about her or where she might be; it hurt to
wonder if she was still alive. To steady himself, to keep pandemonium
at bay, he stared at his hands, studied his palms with their mysterious
lines for a good while.

Finally he laced his fingers together, turned his hands inside out and
stretched them over his head, making a guttural sound, a sound that
meant that his reverie must stop. It was time to leaave, to return to his
busy household in New Lenox.

Hank

When Hank told Ruthie about Felix as they rode their bicycles back to her truck parked at Montrose that Sunday, he told her about the roles Jeanette and Bonnie (though he left out the motel part) and the coroner, and Jerome and Sal and even his living brother, *El Jefe*, had played in the ordeal. Then he told her about something else:

"The strange thing is, I had a premonition the night before (though, of course, I didn't know what it was a premonition of at the time). I had been visiting my friend Arty. He has been a friend since grade school, somebody I have known for a long time. Anyway, we yacked and drank beer until late in the night, or, I should say, early in the morning. Then his wife yelled downstairs for him to come on up and get some sleep—work tomorrow and so on. So, I said my goodbyes. But when I walked out on the stoop, the whole sky lit up. A huge shooting star exploded. I pounded on the door for Arty to come see. He was in his undershorts when he finally got to the door, and in no mood for shooting stars. 'You're crazy,' he said, 'Go home to bed.' So, I left, but I tell you I'd never seen the sky light up like that before. I felt it was signaling something. It woulda been just before or just about the time my brother died, you see."

"That *is* strange, Hank. It'd make me wonder too."

"I'm no Jesus freak, believe me. I don't even believe in God. I'm not one to look for messages in Bible stories or bright stars. But I couldn't help but feel, I don't know, some collision in the universe, some sign? It's stayed with me."

They rode in silence for a while, then Ruthie said, "It's strange. I had a vision when I met you. An image of a painting I once saw flashed through my mind. And now I think it had something to do with you."

"What painting?"

"It was a painting of someone who needed to be left alone because bad things had happened to him."

Hank nodded his head. "You don't know the half of it," he said. "But I have the feeling I'll be telling you everything if I get a chance to see you again."

"Well, of course, you will. Why not?" She smiled wryly. He liked her smile. It seemed to suggest they shared a common joke and a common history, an easy intimacy.

On his way back from Montrose, Hank rode against the wind, exerting all his leg muscles, cringing his face against pin-point attacks by the relentless blowing air. Yet his happy mood carried him along with the ease of the back wind that had transported him and Ruthie to Montrose.

When he got to work on Monday, he checked over his old car very well, inch by inch, inside and out. He wanted to be sure the car was in good working order. He did not want any snags to get in his way to arrive on time in front of the Picasso on the following Sunday.

The two guys Hank worked with at Cash's were young, certified auto repairers, gun enthusiasts and paintball partners who stuck together and showed no respect for Hank's experience. A tension had built up about the distribution of jobs. Hank's assessment was that working together, the two hot shots always seemed to finagle projects that paid well but were not challenging or time consuming, leaving him with those less desirable. The tension about jobs led to other antagonisms, though Hank tried to avoid them, sticking to himself, socializing only with Jeanette or Carl, the Black auto painter, who also usually stuck to himself. Cash was seldom around anymore, and when he did swing by, he only wanted to collect money and hear good news about business.

When the two wisenheimers found out that Hank had had surgery at the county hospital, they started complaining about their taxes: Why did they have to support people who could not make their own way? Hank tried to write them off, calling them in his mind "parts replacers" because, despite their certifications, they did not know how to straighten or contour or weld very well. Still, their off-hand digs got under his skin.

One day, a few months before he met Ruthie, Hank "borrowed" a gun from the glove compartment of the car belonging to Barney, one of the hot shots. He had noticed the small revolver and made note of it a year before and several times since when the faulty compartment door had been left open. Hank knew almost nothing about guns and wasn't particularly interested in them, though he had once kept a .22 rifle with which to shoot the rats that infested Cash's first body shop. He figured he was smart enough and had good enough eye-hand co-ordination to shoot the revolver. The thing was Bugs had been dead a couple of years, and he had done nothing about the revenge he thought Sal deserved. He wanted him to know he had not forgotten. He still suspected foul play had been involved in Felix's death. He carried the gun around for several weeks. He found out where Sal was staying and sometimes staked out his house or followed him when he left the house, biding his time to actually confront him. Hank thought about his brother Bugs a lot. He owed him something. True, Bugs had been a pain in the ass. They often got into fights, even fist fights, but Bugs didn't deserve to die. And since he did die, he deserved to be buried by both of his brothers. Hank drove to the *Jefe's* house late one night, but all the lights were out. He hated Martha. Hated her. He felt the gun in his hand, not so much a weapon to hurt her with, but as a talisman to regain power, to take away the power she had over Samuel. It was her fault that *El Jefe* had stayed away from his brothers.

And then his thoughts returned to Sal. Hank just wanted to hear the truth from Sal. He imagined holding the gun to his head, cocking the hammer. Did Sal think no one cared about Bugs? Did Sal think that he and his brother didn't matter? Those were the questions he would ask when the time was right. But somehow the time never seemed right. So he kept the gun in his pocket.

One Sunday shortly before he met Ruthie, Hank parked his car downtown. When he came back from walking around, it was gone. He started trembling with agitation. He walked to 7-11 to get some cigarettes. He was so jittery he could barely light his cigarette. A bum sitting on the curb asked him for money as Hank walked out of the store. "Somebody just stole my car, Asshole," Hank said. "You think I am going to give you some fucking money?" He took the small revolver out of his jeans pocket and waved it in front of the old guy's face. The bum started wailing as he scrambled away, leaving Hank alone on the sidewalk with a gun in his hand and a cigarette dangling from his mouth. Then Hank almost started making the same wailing sound the bum had made. He hated being out of control. He rambled down the streets, hopelessly looking for his stolen car.

He found it. He had been wrong about where he had parked it. "Shit!" he thought. "Shit, shit, shit." He hated himself for losing control, for being so stupid. He couldn't shake the sound of the bum wailing and it had been his fault. He drove to Burnham Harbor and threw the gun in the lake. He thought to himself, "I was always one for self-defense. I was always one for catch and release." Maybe he was capable of murder when his dark side took control, but maybe not. Either way, the episode was over. But a feeling of failure lingered. He had acted like a bully toward the bum, and he had failed Bugs again. Hank drove the streets downtown slowly, looking for the bum to make amends. Once he spotted him, he slowed down and rolled down a window to talk, but the bum staggered away, a look of full terror on his face.

Back at the shop, Hank realized he could have returned the gun to the glove compartment instead of throwing it in the lake. "Oh, well," he thought. He could not really feel sorry for stealing from his gun-crazy nemeses. For weeks, since the gun went missing, the two hot shots had been eyeing him suspiciously.

The day after the bicycle tour with Ruthie, Hank no longer gave his two work mates any thought. His brush with insanity seemed distant and unrelated to him now, though it had at first sobered him and caused him to be reflective. He had started thinking seriously that he needed someone in his life to keep him calm. Meeting Ruthie had been fortuitous. He would take things with her slowly and carefully; maybe this time with this girl he could make things last. He whistled as he opened the hood to inspect his own jalopy for possible mechanical failures.

At five in the morning that next Sunday he was up and about getting ready to meet Ruthie. He filled a thermos with coffee and packed an extra tin cup for her. He hoped nothing would prevent her from showing up. He recalled the way she listened to him with her dark eyes concerned and curious. She seemed open to try new things, able to match his sense of adventure. He knew it was premature, but he was starting to imagine a life with her, starting to imagine his life without her to be impossible.

Ruthie

It is June, about three weeks after Ruthie and Hank first met, and they are walking in Grant Park when a stranger, probably in his mid-40s, walks up to them. Hank's black sleeveless t-shirt reveals his biceps and flat stomach to an advantage that made Ruthie swallow hard when she first spied him that morning next to his car in front of the Picasso. He is beautiful, she thought as she walked up to him and curved her arm around his shoulder. They are becoming more and more familiar with each other's bodies. A touch here, a hug there; approach, retreat; hide and seek, a sprinkle of flirtation. Will this be the day she brings him home or he, her?

"Hey, Mick. Hey, Mick Jagger," the stranger taunts Hank. It is not only Hank's black t-shirt and his biceps but also Hank's gaunt face and his slight swagger; it is Hank's haircut and his brown hair with light streaks bleached a bit by the sun.

"How're you doing?" Ruthie states, states more than asks, stepping between Hank and the stranger, diverting the stranger's attention, her tone friendly enough, but dismissive too, dismissing the stranger, not really wanting a report on his wellbeing, not really wanting to hear an answer. She and Hank turn away from him and walk over to a huge planter and sit on the edge of it and begin to talk to each other, hands accidently touching, eyes meeting, as they gesture and converse. But the stranger—high perhaps, drunk perhaps, drugged perhaps, un-kempt and unshaven, for sure—wants to be included. He struts over and sits too close to Hank, as if to dominate him. Hank, on principle, does not budge. Danger hovers. Ruthie begins to talk rapidly to diffuse the tension. A cloud of calm descends upon her as she assumes the Malasana squat pose from her "Yoga with Allie" video and as she sees the stranger wipe the blade of a pocketknife on his pants leg and then cut a hangnail.

"We're just exploring the city," she says to keep the stranger focused on her as she leans forward into her squat toward him. The pose keeps her calm, but ready to pounce at the same time. "We were wondering how much the mayor has in his budget for flowers. They're everywhere, right? But gorgeous, right?"

"What do you see in Mickey, here? Why are you with him and not me?" the stranger asks her, changing the subject, pocketknife open in hand, as he bumps up against Hank who still does not budge.

"Oh, we're both into skyscrapers. We're learning all the city buildings together. By the way, I'm Ruthie," Ruthie says, offering the stranger her hand, to dispel the unanswered question. The stranger has no choice but to shake her hand and say his name, which, if he's to be believed, is Woody.

"And I'm Hank," Hank says, following Ruthie's lead, turning determinedly to offer his hand and to inch naturally away from his rival without conceding a retreat.

"Oh, My gosh!" Ruthie exclaims as though she has just thought of something urgent. She leans now in Hank's direction to touch Hank's arm. "Hank, we better get going. I've got to get home by four, remember? Remember the babysitter?" Ruthie prevaricates as she scooches out of her yoga pose and jumps off the wide planter rim onto the ground. "It's been so nice talking to you, Woody. You have a good day," she feigns friendliness as Hank takes his place by her side. They turn and start walking away—not too fast, not too slow. They reach a traffic light at Michigan Avenue before Hank looks back to see if Woody's following. Thankfully, he's not. Not only Hank's hands, but his whole body is shaking as he stops to light a cigarette.

"Thanks," he says. "You handled that well. Look at me, I'm shaking. I was sure I would have to fight the bastard. The guy was full of Dutch courage, beer muscles. But really, Ruthie, you did good."

Ruthie ignores the compliment, not sure she deserves it, not sure what she has even done. Avoiding blow-ups is second nature to her. She honed the skill as a child: a survival tactic in her aunt's house. She wants to kiss Hank, a real kiss on the lips. But the timing is wrong. He's thinking about Woody, not her. He has a cigarette dangling from his mouth and his hands are still shaking and he wants to call it a day.

*

"Meet and greet." These are the words of Allie, the yoga teacher on the video. Ruthie is a bit skeptical of the eastern goodwill that yoga embraces, but she is giving it a try. The video is helping a sprain in her lower back, a result of lifting her bicycle into the back of her pick-up truck, twisting her torso and somehow hurting her back in the process. Allie says, "Tension in our bodies and stressful situations come our way, will always come our way, but how we *meet* them and *greet* them and tend to them is what it is all about." Ruthie agrees. She likes Allie. She thinks, "Meet and greet." It is a kind of mantra.

*

When Ruthie was 16, her aunt almost killed Ruthie's father with a butcher knife. This was not typical behavior on the part of her aunt who usually showed her displeasure by locking herself up in her room and not talking for weeks at a time. Ruthie cannot remember (or maybe never knew) what the fight was about. Her father had left Ruthie with his sister, her aunt, when Ruthie's mother died shortly after Ruthie's birth. Her aunt, Aunt Marge, was at the time of this dumping of motherless Ruthie already caring for her own parents, both of whom were elderly and disabled, so Ruthie arrived as a resented burden.

Her father seldom came around. He rented a room in Oak Lawn, close to the hospital where he worked in the purchasing department. Ruthie had only been to his room once. She took note of the empty Scotch bottles lining the window sill and the window itself, which was dirty and had no blinds or curtains to get in the way of the bottles.

The weird thing is that the image Ruthie remembers is of her father on the floor, her aunt straddling him, her rump in the air, the knife next to his throat. Wouldn't her father have been stronger than her aunt? And where were her grandparents? Amid this chaotic scene, a calm had descended upon Ruthie. She picked up the wall phone in the hall and announced with perfect tranquility that she was going to call the police.

"Don't you dare!" her father yelled from the floor, more scared of the exposure and embarrassment than his impending death.

Ruthie dialed some random numbers and feigned the call, loudly enunciating her address, clear enough to disengage her aunt who was soon standing, the knife at her side. "You are going nowhere," her aunt said to her father, who was scrambling to his feet. "We will both be here when they come." By the time Ruthie admitted to them that she had not really called the police, the argument had dissipated and her father got ready to leave.

Two years later, Ruthie herself left her aunt's house with a scholarship to study at the teaching college in Normal, Illinois and then, after she graduated, she left forever to find teaching jobs overseas, following some romantic notion cultivated by novels she read and inspired by two college boyfriends, deemed "foreign students," in the lingo of the day—boyfriends who helped her pronounce greetings and gratitude in French and Arabic correctly and who opened up her world to imagine an expansive future for herself.

Now she seldom visits her father and her aunt. From a distance, she has a certain sympathy for them: for her aunt, who, Ruthie now realizes, never had an opportunity to have a life of her own, who was cast into a never-ending role of caregiver, even now caring for her alcoholic brother, Ruthie's father; and a certain sympathy for her father, who, as a young man of 23, had lost his wife and had been too overwhelmed to raise his daughter. Yes, from a distance, she can see all of this objectively and even with compassion. But close up, she only grows restless and angry at the narrow routines her aunt and father obey. "Why would anyone want to leave the neighborhood?" Ruthie can imagine them wondering. No matter how Ruthie frames the past, she is its trouble at the center.

*

Meet and greet. Calm at the center. It is time to make it happen. The sun is already bouncing off the concrete at Daley Plaza this Sunday morning. More than a month has gone by since she first met Hank. She has seen him every Sunday morning since. This morning when she greets him at the Picasso, she not only encircles his shoulder with her arm, but kisses his cheek and then his lips. He kisses her back.

"Hello, Beautiful!" he smiles, putting his arm around her waist.

They hold hands as they set out to explore the city with silent promises to start a new life for themselves together.

Caleb

Caleb's father came to his high school graduation, which was only the second time Caleb ever remembered seeing his father, Samuel, in his entire life. After the ceremony and before the party that Caleb's cousin Rocio and his aunt Celia prepared, Samuel took him for a ride, and they talked. His father seemed very serious and honest, as though wanting to settle a debt with him.

"I know life must've been tough for you," Samuel began. "Your mother died when you were young, and I never was a father for you. I myself came from not a normal family. I lost my mother and father too, though not quite as young as you. I'm sorry. I should've tried. But it's been so complicated, you know with another family, and my wife would not be one to invite you into our home. She's so protective of her own children." Samuel paused and then asked, "What do you know about me? What did your mother tell you about me?"

"Lots of stuff. She told me that you did not go to Vietnam. You never joined the military."

"That's true. Did she hold it against me?"

"No, she wouldn't of. I don't either, even though I've joined up myself."

"So I heard."

"My cousin's husband says the army will give me a sense of direction. I did poorly in school in some subjects, the ones that required lots of reading."

"My brother Hank was like that too. But he was very good at math and good at fixing things. What else did your mother tell you about me?"

"She and you used to help the priest at church."

"Yes," Samuel laughed, "we did work for a priest and had fun doing it, too." Then he paused before he said, "Caleb, I never knew you were coming. I never knew until after you were born and by that time, I was going to marry my wife."

"I sent you a couple of letters, but I never got any answers."

"I got 'em, Caleb. I saved 'em. I still have them. I read them again before I came here. I'm sorry I never answered them. I won't give you any lame excuses. I'm sorry. When I heard you were graduating from high school, I thought, 'I should talk to him.'"

After a long, mostly friendly, conversation, Caleb's father had to catch a plane to Chicago. He said that he was sorry he was not able to attend the graduation party, but he gave Caleb an envelope before he left. Caleb found a card and a check for 1,000 dollars in the envelope. The strange thing was the card was a photograph postcard with a picture of Samuel's other children, a photo of their whole family. Their names were printed on the back. On the front were the typeset words "Greetings from the Stone Family." His father had written him a note below the names on the back, "Hi, Caleb. Congratulations on your graduation. All the best!" He also wrote the ages and order of birth of his five other children above their names.

Caleb did not know what to make of it. What was the message? A warning? "Remember, I have another family. I cannot be your father." Or a plea for understanding? "Here is my family. They are important to me, so I share them with you." Or a rejection? "This is my real family. You are just my bastard son. Take the thousand dollars and do not bother me again." Caleb tried but found no means by which the message could be construed as encouragement, by which the photo was the welcoming invitation he was hoping for to join his paternal family. He put it in his backpack next to another letter and a ring that he had meant to show his father. But he had been more concerned about the letters his father had never written him. He had forgotten about Glad-ys' letter and ring.

*

Caleb was in the army for six years. He was deployed to the Iraq War after 9/11. He worked in an EOD unit in Iraq. His job was to help clear roads and buildings of IEDs, explosive devices, and although he was not the one who disassembled the IEDs, he and the others in the unit expe-rienced almost daily blasts at close range. He later learned that the explo-sive waves, traveling through his brain at high velocity, caused damage: memory loss, impairments solving problems, and making decisions.

After he served in Iraq, he served in Afghanistan. There he was in a Humvee when a car bomb went off, injuring his foot. Fortunately, sur-gery saved his foot, but even now, two years later, he sometimes needed to walk with a cane. "Gimpy" his fellow soldiers, some of whom were gimpy too, called him. He wrote his father several times, but never received an answer back.

*

When his deployment to Afghanistan was over, he decided not to re-enlist, but he was not sure what to do with his life. By this time, his Aunt Celia had died, and his cousin Rocio and her husband had three children of their own to worry about.

He thought he might try going to Chicago. Caleb had some cousins he did not know very well in Chicago, and he had a close friend named Washington or Wash, as they called him, with whom he had served in Afghanistan, and he had his father, Samuel.

Samuel's words had been frank and kind when they talked after Caleb's high school graduation. Caleb did not understand why his fa-

ther, after sharing with him such an intimate conversation, had not answered his letters, sent at a time when he, Caleb, had been very lonely
and in danger—when he had been fighting wars. Caleb needed an explanation, maybe a confrontation; he needed to quell life-long resent-
ments that so often rose to the surface in a fit of unpredictable anger.
So Caleb went to Chicago, and one fall day accompanied by Wash for
moral support, came to knock on the door of his father's family home
in Will County on Meadow Lark Lane in New Lennox, Illinois.

Hank

Hank left the house before Ruthie awoke. He had always been able to wake up without an alarm clock just by telling himself the night before the time he needed to be up, which was 3 o'clock or 4 o'clock in the morning now most days. Hank was working at Benny's again, a matter of concern to Ruthie. "Why would you go back to someone who kicked you when you were down?" Ruthie asked. Hank just shrugged his shoulders. Ruthie thought he held too much in without protest or retaliation, but he knew that if he allowed every injustice he encountered to bother him, he would end up exploding and probably in jail. His expectations of others synced with his understanding of randomness in the universe. People could not be counted on.

"I've had it with the two hot shots at Cash's," he explained, "and Benny has a straightening job that only I can do." Hank was quite sure Benny, obtuse and unreflective, didn't even remember the conditions under which Hank left his garage years before.

Hank was living with Ruthie in a row house near Lawler Park on the Southwest side. They bought the house when Ruthie inherited some money when her aunt died, giving them enough for a down payment. They would still go downtown occasionally on Sunday mornings to look at buildings, but four years had passed since they first started doing so, and they had slowly drifted in new directions.

As an offshoot of their architecture mission, he and Ruthie had once gone on a nature walk at Lincoln Park led by Derrick Peterson, a man they met while downtown one day, looking down at a hole in the ground, the would-be foundation of a new skyscraper. Derrick explained that although he, like them, made a point to investigate new buildings going up, his real passion was nature. He led bird walks at both Lincoln Park and Jackson Park and invited them to join him the following Sunday at Lincoln Park. He told them on the walk that over 400 birds could be found in Illinois and he pointed out a flicker tapping a tree and noted the call of a golden-crowned kinglet. Hank, ever the reader of nature, realized here was a whole new chapter to master. He went on several more walks with Derrick and then explored Montrose Harbor and Jackson Park, hooking up with the best birders during the spring migration. No matter the task at hand, he liked to challenge himself by competing with those with the best reputation. He had a lot of catching up to do, for some of the best had been honing their skills since childhood and Hank was approaching the age of fifty.

Hank was becoming an expert and addicted birder. He liked to get a few hours in before work at the Portage National Heritage Site, the place Marquette and Joliet foraged on their short cut home from exploration, a very historical spot, but long neglected in those days when Hank started to scout it, hoping to spot a warbler or "hunt" down the distant call of a great horned owl, just before the sun rose. It was the hunt that attracted him to birding, just as it had drawn him to fishing: figuring out natural habitat and animal habits tested some of his best skills.

Having had a brush with death, Hank was motivated more than ever to follow his curiosity and restless spirit. He couldn't take life for granted. The brain tumor had reminded him uncomfortably of his father's mental illness, and Hank's secret fear was that he might have inherited his father's disease. After the operation, he was administered morphine for residual pain, but had not been told the type of medicine nor warned of side effects. When he started seeing cartoon figures dancing before his eyes, he told himself he would now have to live a more careful, circumscribed life, questioning everything he saw before him, but was willfully resolved not to go completely crazy or mis-tell reality.

Fortunately, a doctor eventually explained to him that he was suffering the side effects of morphine. The same doctor told him that he might suffer short-term memory loss and seizures due to scarring. The operation could not remove the entire tumor, the doctor said, because it entwined with his optic nerve. It was a slow-growing tumor, but eventually another operation would be needed. So far, Hank had not noticed any side effects, but he stayed vigilant, took seizure medication, tried not to drink too much, tried unsuccessfully not to smoke, and could often be seen doing chin-ups in Lawler Park.

*

Hank soon learned that among the best birders were two older women. Because they were retired, they could bird during the day on weekdays, and because Hank occasionally had days off when business was slow, he would catch up with them and pick their brains to learn all he could. After he met Sylvia at Montrose, he described her to Ruthie: "A little old lady bird watcher. You would think of her that way—a bird *watcher*—if you saw her with her straw hat and tennis shoes and bicycle. In a way her name *Sylvia* fits her because she has this slow, precise way of pronouncing words. Well, I can't explain it—Sylvia of the silver tongue. She's got to be in her late seventies, but she can still hear fairly well."

Sylvia gave away a religious paper called *Awake,* but after a while she stopped trying to get Hank to take it. "I am not religious," he told her. "Jesus? Mohammed? Pro-choice? Pro-life? Forget it. Talk birds to me." Sylvia laughed. Hank also met Sakura at Montrose. She was a Japanese woman in her early 60s who knew as much about birds, Hank told Ruthie, as any of the men ornithologists "who swaggered and spouted knowledge at Montrose on the weekends."

That day, instead of going to Portage, Hank met up with Sylvia and Sakura on the north side where the two women lived. Sakura drove them to Momence Field in Kankakee County. She drove with her left foot for the brake and her right foot for the gas, but Hank noted she was very aware of her surroundings. She knew what was going on around her, so, despite her strange foot work, Hank relaxed as he rode next to her. He liked birding with Sakura because she only called a bird when she was sure she had correctly identified it. At Jackson Park one day, she had called a black-throated blue warbler. The "hot shots" of the local birding world questioned her call, saying none had been spotted yet that year. However, she was able to lead them to a deciduous patch of trees where the male could be heard singing its shrill song, "I am so lazzzy" in the understory.

At Momence Field only two sparrows were calling, the Vesper sparrow and the Henslow's sparrow, providing a great chance to distinguish those two calls. Later in the day they saw a blue grosbeak. It was a very hot July day and they were birding in fields with little shade. The sun was merciless and Sakura kept asking Sylvia if she would like to sit down, but Sylvia was a real trooper, determined to keep up with her two younger companions. The sparrows and grosbeak were lifers for Hank, meaning that this was his first sighting of those birds. Sakura had seen them before as she often birded in Kankakee County. Hank was not sure if they were lifers for Sylvia, but he wondered about it later after he learned what happened to her.

At the end of August, Sakura called and left a message on his answering machine about Sylvia. The day after their trip, Sylvia got up, pedaled her bicycle a quarter mile along the lake to Montrose, birded a very short while, returned home within an hour, sat in a chair, fell asleep, and died peacefully. That was the gist of the message Sakura left on the answering machine. Sakura had been asking around for weeks,

"Has anyone seen Sylvia?" Finally, she found someone who had heard of her death, and so she shared the news with Hank. She feared that their exhausting trip the day before led to her death.

*

Hank, Benny, and another worker, Wayne, were listening to the radio when the planes crashed into the World Trade Center. Benny then turned on the television. They saw the towers come down. Hank was truly amazed at the way they collapsed. When he and Ruthie had explored the buildings downtown, he would ask lots of questions anytime he got a chance to talk to a construction worker or maintenance worker. "I would have thought the fireproofing would have kept them up," he told the others. "That just shows you how hot it got." Later, Wayne said, "We should bomb them." But Hank thought, "Yeah, right, like who, Hamster Brain?" Then an announcer on the television said, "It's a wake-up call." That got Hank thinking about Sylvia.

"Dead, not awake," he thought (sleeping in a chair with *Awakes* stacked all over the room, screaming their hysterical headlines). Dead just a little while, dying before she knew that men would drive a plane right into a skyscraper. It was then that he wondered if the Vesper sparrow and the Henslow's sparrow and the blue grosbeak were lifers for her. Lifers the day before she died.

"People tell themselves stories," Hank told Ruthie. "There's no way Sakura could know that Sylvia died peacefully. Maybe Sylvia had an excruciatingly painful heart attack and was very frightened the seconds before she died."

"Maybe," Ruthie assented. "I guess stories, though, help us get through losses."

"I'd rather know the truth," Hank said, suddenly visibly upset. Ruthie was about to respond, but he said, "End of conversation." It was what he always said when he could no longer converse calmly. He walked down the stairs to the basement, his refuge, thinking about Sakura's message. Sakura was afraid they had killed Sylvia because they had stayed out birding in the hot sun for so long. The 'died peacefully' just eased her conscience, he thought. He wanted to know the truth about things, about everything—Sylvia, sure, but all the more about Bugs and his mother. He didn't need wake-up calls. He didn't tell himself stories or offer himself platitudes to feel better. He was awake. "Shit," he thought, "I don't even need a ticking alarm clock to wake me up in morning."

Martha

When Martha opened the door, two young men with dark skin stood before her. One had the features of an African American and one had the features of her very own husband. She felt confused and dizzy, reaching for the door frame to steady herself. Ordinarily she would have said, "May I help you?" but "What do you want?" came from her lips. They wanted to see her husband. She nodded yes, totally flummoxed, though from a certain perspective, their request seemed more than reasonable because so did she want to see her husband. "You wait here. Stay right here," she said, allowing them to stand in the foyer, but not offering to take their jackets, nor to find them chairs. She stumbled into the kitchen to call Samuel on the wall phone, and then without speaking to them again, she retreated to her bedroom upstairs to lie down. Her head pounded with unwelcome knowledge she had not yet fully processed. Her stomach churned with the consequences of that knowledge. And as she lay on the bed, the ceiling swirled above her.

In the distance, an hour or so later, she heard Samuel come in the front door and then heard the rumblings of a conversation she could not make out. She lay in a fetal position, hoping Samuel would enter the bedroom and make her anxiety go away. Instead, when he finally came into the room and spoke to her, he told her that Caleb would be staying with them for a while. He could not and would not turn him away. Caleb had been wounded fighting in a war. He had nowhere else to go. "I will help him find a place. It won't be for long," he said. "With Madeline and Steve away at college, we've got plenty of room."

"He can't stay in Steve's room. He cannot stay at all," Martha cried.

"He can stay in the guest bedroom in the basement. There's a bathroom down there. He won't bother you at all," Samuel said. And with a sinking feeling, Martha knew she could not win the argument.

"I don't feel well," she said. She stumbled to her feet and went into the master bathroom and threw up. "He'll never be a part of my family," she called from the bathroom before she retched again.

*

Martha's illness did not begin the day Caleb arrived. Several years earlier she started experiencing dizzy spells and unexpected falls. Trying to make light of the problem, Samuel, who had been reprogramming computers at work for the upcoming year 2000, teased her, saying that she had not been programmed for the New Millennium and was experiencing the Y2K bug. However, when the issue persisted, he helped her seek medical opinions. Eventually, she was given an MRI to see if demyelination of the nerves had occurred, a definite sign of multiple sclerosis. The MRI found no irregularities, but the doctor pointed out that the symptoms were typical of patients with MS. He said that her condition might be psychogenic.

"I am not faking this," Martha protested.

"No, of course not," said the doctor. "But there's a strong connection between the mind and the body. Sometimes depression or tension can cause symptoms even though tests do not show disease. Have you been upset or worried lately?"

Martha took a moment to assess her emotional state. "Well, my husband and I didn't agree about having another child."

"You already have five children?"

"Well, yes," Martha said. "I do have five children, but we can afford them. I have taken very good care of them. My mother helps me. They all do well in school. My two youngest are excellent athletes."

"Well, perhaps you're going through a transition period," the doctor said, "a time of life when we search for a new purpose; perhaps this is causing tension and worry. However, ordinary tension and worry do not usually affect our bodies in such an extreme way. Have you had trauma in your life?"

Martha thought for a minute. "Well, my father died when I was nine, and, of course, that was traumatic. Also, I had a twin who died in the womb before I was born. I wouldn't even have known about it if my mother had not told me. But even so, ever since I found out, I ache for her. It is strange to say, but even before I found out, I ached for her. I felt her absence. Maybe that doesn't make sense, but it's what I feel and felt."

"I see," the doctor said. "You felt a loss and then perhaps, you felt survivor's guilt. I am not sure exactly what's going on. I'm not a psychologist, but perhaps you should see one to help us understand. This disease may or may not have a psychological component. We'll treat the symptoms for now and keep searching for diagnosis."

The conversation with the doctor at that time (a few years before Caleb rang her doorbell and disrupted her life even more) caused Martha to start thinking about her fear of separation. She thought about Casper and Sally, her youngest children, both of whom were captains of their soccer teams. She went to nearly all their games and cheered them on, admiring the deftness with which they played. Casper's coach had told her that Casper had real leadership qualities, while Sally's coach admired her inventiveness and awareness. Martha could not help but note as her young children's physical prowess and grace grew, hers shrank. She felt pride and resentment at the same time. Life, from then on, she realized, would involve separation after separation. Her oldest children would be off to college. Madeline already had a serious boyfriend. Her daughter Sophia had bonded with her music teacher, wanting to emulate her talent on the piano, and seldom had time for

Martha's advice. Her younger children no longer depended on her to play with them or to form their opinions. They had their own friends and activities and thoughts. Martha had always hated separation and change. She had spent years longing for her father and her sister. She stayed close to her mother. She and Samuel had lived with her mother when they first married, and when they were ready to move on, Martha insisted that her mother move with them.

Martha knew and felt secure and proud that Samuel admired and depended on her strong sense of family, kindling his fierce loyalty to her. She was everything his mother had not been, which meant, in his mind, that she would never desert him and in her mind, that she held a certain power and that he would never desert her. Unlike his mother, Martha would never casually have a drink with another man in a bar or take a job that kept her away from her children or forget to shop for food or fail to prepare a meal. She did not understand how any woman could abandon her children. Nevertheless, the security and loyalty that Martha shared with Samuel needed constant vigilance. It did not build her confidence. It did not always ease her unease.

*

Caleb did stay out of Martha's way. He'd usually leave early in the morning to look for work or go to a support group. He would come back late at night and go directly down into the basement. He did not eat meals with the family. Still, Samuel had to tell the children who Caleb was. Still, the resemblance between Caleb and Samuel would be worthy of neighborly comment. All this grated Martha's nerves. She started using a walker. She and Samuel moved to a first-floor bedroom, so she would not have to climb stairs. And then suddenly one day, a new symptom manifested itself: hyperekplexia, a severe startle reflex, sometimes caused her to stiffly fall over backwards when she heard an unexpected sound. The first few times it happened, Samuel again tried to make light of it, kidding her, saying he would buy her a football helmet to protect her head. But one time when she burned herself with hot oil while she was cooking, they both realized the severity of the problem. Again, the doctor ran tests, but could not make a definite diagnosis.

*

Martha would remind Samuel that he had promised he would find Caleb a place of his own to live. Focusing on his mental and physical health problems, attending weekly group therapy, Caleb hadn't found a job yet and Samuel did not see the urgency to make a change. However, as Martha's dissatisfaction grew, Samuel relented. He found a studio apartment for Caleb in Chicago, not far from his support group. He paid the deposit and two months' rent. "You'll have to find a job and pay rent within two months," he told Caleb. He shook Caleb's hand, as though dismissing him, but then he shook his own head with regret. He had started to feel a bond with Caleb, but he just did not have time for bonds outside those of his immediate family with Martha.

Ruthie

Ruthie loved setting up the house and designing the flower beds and vegetable gardens in the yard. She set up bird feeders and a birdbath. She bought a hand lawnmower and pruning shears. She collected water from the rainspouts and composted organic waste. Hank said they needed a cat to catch mice, so they adopted one from the Anti-cruelty Society. Dolly, their gray cat, not only hunted mice, but gradually became an affectionate member of their household, a clown who could diffuse tensions.

Sometimes Hank would go grocery shopping to look for a stewing chicken, and then he would stay up late at night in the kitchen trying to duplicate Gladys's long-ago chicken soup recipe and would wake Ruthie up when it was ready, enthused to share his culinary feat. Ruthie, drowsy and not very hungry, tried hard to match his exuberance as she lifted a spoon of soup to her lips, he standing next to her smiling expectantly. "Mmm," she managed to say, before she shuffled off back to bed.

*

"Be aware of your surroundings!" he would always preach, a lesson for Ruthie who tended to daydream and to live in her own head. One time when she was driving, and he was riding along with her, she had left her windshield wipers on long after it had stopped raining. Eventually she turned them off. "I didn't say anything," Hank said, "because I wanted to see how long it'd take you to realize it had stopped raining.

It was exactly twenty-one minutes."

"I know," Ruthie laughed, finishing his thought, "I was not aware of my surroundings." Hank just shrugged his shoulders and raised the palms of his hands with bemusement.

*

Noli me tangere came and went. They each had their own private spaces in the house, places to retreat to when living or sleeping with another human-being seemed too difficult or when they just needed time to pursue their own interests privately. However, summer evenings, Ruthie would take Hank's hand and walk with him around the yard to show him each new bloom and blossom or baby cucumber or miniature tomato. He mentioned that his mother had planted four o'clocks in their front yard in Cicero one summer and they came back every year from seed. Ruthie bought four o'clock seeds the next day, dug up the grass near the front window, spread dirt and scattered the seeds, which bloomed red, yellow, and white blossoms later that summer.

On one of their walks in the yard, Ruthie noted that the moon was in the west early in the evening. "I don't understand the moon at all," she said. "Sometimes it comes up over there at sunset and sometimes over there. And maybe at one time in my life I understood why we can never see the dark side of the moon. Maybe some teacher taught me that in grammar school, but I've totally forgotten."

"I'll show you," he said and grabbed her hands. "The lawn chair is the earth and we are the moon orbiting the earth but rotating on our own axis too." He started twirling around with her while walking sideways in a circle at the same speed. You see if we twirl and walk at the same speed, our same side always faces the lawn chair." Delighted with the demonstration and drunk with the beauty of the night sky, Ruthie couldn't stop laughing.

"I sorta understand," she said.

"And sometimes the moon is with us during the day, but we don't see it. We only see it when the sun goes down, and that's why we see it in the West at sunset. But it's setting, not rising. It's not on a twenty-four-hour schedule like the sun." They were still twirling and only stopped when Ruthie freed her hands from his and hugged him. "Thank you!" she said, kissing his cheek. They walked back to the house arm in arm, comrades and lovers in arms, a visible sliver of the moon setting in the West.

*

Ruthie had for many years enjoyed drawing and oil painting not from models or nature, but from photographs, experimenting by distorting set poses or making unexpected additions to a composition or adding inappropriate color. She so admired Andy Warhol's photographic-silk screen of the green-faced Marilyn Monroe! Lately, Ruthie had gotten interested in "the gaze" in photography: photographs from the *National Geographic* taken by white photographers, showing native peoples as exotic and strange, or family photographs taken by a father with posed blond daughters dressed in pleated navy-blue skirts and knee socks, surrounded by all the trappings of privilege: paintings, books, oriental rugs on the floor, a fire blazing in the fireplace.

Ruthie would choose a photograph, paint it faithfully, and then add details to draw attention to the "gaze" from which it was taken. She might add large black freckles on an otherwise unblemished white face or add a dark ghost hovering over a tranquil domestic scene. She might change the titles of the books on a shelf or paint in a complacent photographer, photographing a victim of war in a third-world country. Ruthie knew she was a novice, but she was inspired by the possibilities and treasured her time alone imagining them.

She thought to herself that one reason she had been able to stay with Hank for so long was not only because she loved him and felt his love, but because he left her alone to daydream, to paint, to go out, to be herself without questions. She liked to think she extended him the same freedom, though sometimes she found herself uncomfortable with his closeness to Bonnie and her family. It bothered her that it bothered her. In many ways, she and Hank still functioned as single people, and she wanted to preserve that, be proud that they could forge a new way and not rely on convention. "Friends with benefits" was the joke of the day, replete with sexual innuendo, overheard again as Ruthie rode the bus one day with several women returning home from office jobs at Nabisco.

A few years after they moved into the house, Hank went to the doctor for a follow-up MRI. Dr. Ramirez told him that his tumor was growing back, but slowly. Since Hank had not had any seizures, he could now stop taking the seizure medicine. Freed of the medication, Hank felt more secure drinking socially. At first, Ruthie saw no harm. She enjoyed talking with friends over a drink and welcomed this as a new social activity to share with Hank. Over time, though, Hank began drinking more, buying a case of beer almost every week. In the past, he had always filled a thermos with coffee, milk, and sugar and took swigs compulsively all day long as he worked or birded or watched television, but now beer became his compulsive drink of choice.

Ever the helpful missionary, Ruthie thought that if she could help him ameliorate some of his past sorrows, he might not drink excessively. She had long thought that they should return to Wisconsin and finally retrieve the ashes of his brother Felix. Hank had mentioned showing her the flowage area when they first met. However, they had never gone, and Hank seldom mentioned the drowning accident anymore, or when he did, he did so angrily, regretful that he had never sought the revenge he mistakenly felt Felix's companions deserved. Ruthie hesitated to bring up the idea of finally burying the ashes: maybe it would end up being more upsetting than helpful. She also found the task easy to postpone, preoccupied as she was by the routines of earning a living and taking care of the house, the yard, the cat.

One day, however, Hank did bring up Gladys again, saying he wished he could have just said goodbye to her. He described his feeling "as the nightmare I can never wake up from," the break in his voice adding poignancy to his words. Moments before, he had grabbed a beer from the fridge and was walking back downstairs to watch a football game. He had stopped on a stair and turned around, pivoting on the ball of his foot to turn toward the kitchen to tell her as she stood cooking at the stove at the top of the stairs. She remembered finding the timing strangely inappropriate for such emotional communication. He might have told her when they were having a long serious conversation in the living room, or when they sat together in lawn chairs on the patio in the evenings after their walk around the yard. But he told her as he was leaving the kitchen, walking down the stairs, as though it had just occurred to him, as if he were only reminding her of a detail that he had forgot to mention. The incident, the pain in his voice, stayed with her.

Ruthie had become quite skilled at finding old friends from nearly all the continents of the earth on the Internet. She thought Gladys might very well be dead, being past 80 by then. Ruthie was determined to find out something about her. She started searching obituaries and white pages.

Success was easier than she might have expected. Her first break was finding a site sponsored by the Social Security department, which published lists of deaths by name and social security numbers. She looked up *Gladys O'Brien* and then *Gladys Stone*. She found the death of a Gladys Stone the age of Hank's mother in Florida. The social security card of this Gladys Stone had been issued in Illinois, which made sense, because Gladys had probably gotten her first salaried job when she started working at Western Union; there probably had not been a real reason to get a social security card in South Dakota before then.

So, Gladys had stayed in Florida? The site gave the town where she had died. When Ruthie looked up the town called Davie on a map, she found that it was not far from the Gulfstream racetrack. Gladys had died almost exactly where Hank had dropped her off years before! With the information gleaned from the Internet sites, Ruthie was finally able to locate two brief obituaries: one published in the *Fort Lauderdale Sentinel* and one published in the *Miami Herald*. They both read the same, the bare minimum: date of death, age at death (80), residence, and burial site.

Ruthie was not sure what to do with this information. She wanted to tell Hank but did not know how to broach the subject. One evening as they walked around the yard together, she quietly told him that she had searched for his mother on the Internet and had found some information. He nodded his head but did not seem overly curious to know what she had found. However, Ruthie felt determined to finish what she had so tremulously started to say and told him all that she had learned. He nodded his head again but did not comment. Ruthie felt as though he had not heard her. But, of course, he had. He did not seem upset. Ruthie could not characterize his reaction at all. His face was blank, as though he were thinking of something else. As though where his mother had died, or even where she had lived for the past 40 years was not relevant, was not the point. And maybe, after all, it wasn't. The conversation turned to another topic. They never spoke about Ruthie's Internet find again.

*

Meanwhile the years went by, one and then another. Ruthie worried about Hank's drinking and worried about the tumor that was growing inside his head. Her worry shaded the bright joys of gardening and domesticity that she had at first enjoyed without worry. The ticking clock, which Hank said he did not need to wake him up, had no need for him either, absolutely no need for anyone. It just kept ticking away no matter what.

Bonnie

It had been going on for several years now. A long remission and then a return with his condition worsening, and then remission again. Theo had been diagnosed with lymphoma and now in the year 1998, he would soon die. That was a medical fact. Her husband was in the hospital dying of lymphoma. Bonnie saw him every morning, every break, and in the evenings after work. He was no longer conscious. She had to decide when to pull the plug. Of course, she was a nurse and was used to being matter of fact about such matters. The face she showed the world was sensible and unemotional. Some of her colleagues tried to offer support, but she wanted no one to compliment her devotion or feel sorry for her. She wanted everyone to be quiet and leave her alone. Meanwhile, she took up knitting. It was something she could do while she sat with Theo and spoke to him softly, mostly about the kids, and about her patients, and about knitting.

I remember my mother used to knit. Remember that crazy ski cap I wore in junior high? That was my mother's doing, and those reindeer sweaters for Christmas? I swore I would never knit. But now I find it very relaxing. I know you are surprised I am not reading. You always teased me for reading too much. I always loved to read. I thought about becoming an English teacher, but nursing school after marriage seemed more practical. Even in first grade. Hank would come over and listen to me read aloud. Don't be jealous. No, you never are. Anyway, I could tell you had a crush on that Mexican girl who lived in the upstairs apartment in the Stone house. It seemed everyone did. Theo, I know you love me. You know I love you. But honestly, Theo, I can't stay focused. That's why I knit, knit, knit. The repeti-

tion keeps me centered and mindful. It's like reciting the rosary.

She thought that maybe she would like to have a rosary vigil the night before the funeral. She thought she might knit Theo a pair of socks to wear to his funeral. She didn't mention these thoughts aloud to him though.

*

Hank had just moved in with Ruthie but found himself at Bonnie's house several nights a week to offer companionship to the boys while Bonnie stayed late with Theo in the hospital. He made them peanut butter and jelly sandwiches almost every night for supper, though once Ruthie sent him over with a casserole. The night Bonnie finally decided to take Theo off life support, she came back home tear-streaked, yet robotic. Bonnie recounted what had happened almost mechanically while Hank, sitting in a chair in her room, listened to her as she lay exhausted on the bed. Her words drifted as she dozed off. They both slept a few hours, Hank eventually transporting himself in a stupor from the chair to the bed, Bonnie murmuring in her sleep, "knit, knit, purl, purl"—and then half awake, half asleep, following the incipient pattern established in an inexpensive Wisconsin motel, they comforted each other weeping their way slowly and uncertainly to making love, a strange keening that mingled their anguish for Theo with the remembered anguish for Felix and for their departed parents and for a long line of the unknown dead, for the sorry and sorrowful human condition; they strove to reenact that long-ago comfort found in a cheap motel room with the mediocre painting of a clown on the wall—they wade in the grief: knee deep, thigh deep, waist deep—up to the chest, the neck, over the head, submerged in sorrow.

For several days thereafter, Hank stumbled from the house he shared with Ruthie to the house he was now sharing with Bonnie and her sons

and then back again. He missed work. He brought Ruthie to the funeral, and then they drove Bonnie, the boys, and Bonnie's sister to the
airport to fly to San Diego where the sister lived. The sad tryst was over.
Hank turned his full attention to Ruthie whom he was afraid he might
be losing, though she remained in the dark about the specifics, left to
imagine the call and response of a grief that had excluded her.

In a month's time Bonnie and her sons were back home, but Hank
kept his distance from them for a while, and Bonnie did not call. Eventually Will telephoned, asking Hank to watch him practice a new skating routine, and that soon got things back on an even keel. Hank and
the boys skated and hiked and fished and drove around critiquing other drivers, allowing Bonnie time to find the balance in her new life as a
widow and as a single mother with two boys who lost their father and
allowing a way for her and Hank to refigure their friendship, to find its
proper shape and distance and boundaries.

Martha

"My beautiful daughters. I love them so much," Martha wrote as a caption beneath a photograph of Madeline, Sophie, and Sally dressed in party dresses on her Facebook page. Martha loved her children with all her heart and all her soul, and she told them so all the time. She loved her mother, and she loved her husband—and that love within the family circle along with the love of God, she always believed, was all anybody should need.

She and Samuel agreed that the children should go to college, the girls as well as the boys, but by the same token, she wanted her daughters to be beautiful, to marry, to have as strong a sense of family as she herself and Samuel had—and she hoped that when they did marry, they would live nearby—the family circle would expand, of course, to include the beloved mates of her children and the beloved children of her children, the grandchildren.

In part her wishes were coming true. Her daughters were beautiful with her sense of the beautiful. Their blond hair fell to their shoulders; they wore stylish, but modest, clothes, preferring dresses more than jeans or slacks; in professional photographs they transmitted flawless images of unmitigated happiness: smiles with perfect teeth. (Sometimes Samuel thought, when he looked at their smiles in the photos, how much he had paid the orthodontist for them.) Her smiling sons were handsome and tall, and the girlfriends and wives they chose beamed out the same Nordic beauty that her daughters radiated. However, all of Martha's children had decided, with Samuel's blessing, to go to Catholic colleges far from home, and as they finished their studies, all but Steve were starting to settle in those far-flung places. Martha grieved their absences and insisted that she and Samuel visit each twice a year, an undertaking that got increasingly more difficult with Martha's illness. The brood came to visit her, too, of course, but not nearly as often as she would have liked. Their absence, along with her illness, put her in a depressed state of mind. One of her doctors prescribed Prozac, but its supposed miracle effects left her wanting.

Several times during their marriage, she and Samuel confided in Father Peter, the pastor of their church, and she did so now. He suggested that she join a women's group at the parish, a group called *Walking with a Purpose.* When he said *Walking with a Purpose,* she was reminded of Brother Alex from long ago at the Youth Ministry and his idea of "walking" in love.

"Will I really have to go on walks?" Martha asked anxiously, her walker by the side of her chair as she talked with her confessor.

"No, no, of course not," Father Peter assured her with a smile. "Mostly you will sit. You will read scripture and discuss it with other women in the Parish. You can volunteer to sit at literature tables, if you want, at Pro-Life events. Mostly you will just socialize, maybe meet new friends."

Martha had always thought of herself as pro-life personally, but not politically. She was not very political at all. She did not like the idea of harassing women in front of clinics, and she was not ready to do so. However, perhaps she would benefit from socializing with other women in her parish. Samuel was always after her to find a hobby, to find distractions to ease her worries, to take her mind off her disabilities, for her anxiety caused her to call him too often when he was gone from the house. Since he retired and they both got cell phones, her worrying about him when he left to do an errand or visit a friend had gotten worse and her check-up calls more frequent and frenzied. Sometimes she feared he had a car accident or a heart attack. Sometimes she feared he was secretly visiting Caleb and not telling her in order to avoid an argument.

These days, he left her less and less often alone (indeed, he stopped visiting his friends altogether), but she knew her behavior might cause him to resent her and she longed for peace of mind. They had even discussed the issue with a psychiatrist her doctor recommended—the one who had given her the Prozac. The psychiatrist had her do an exercise in which she meditated and did breathing exercises between calls, trying gradually to lengthen the wait time between each call to her husband, the hoped-for end result being that she not panic when Samuel was gone, that she would stop imagining catastrophes. The experiment helped a bit but was not entirely successful in relieving her anxiety and crying fits, nor in ending her compulsion to call.

The women at *Walking with a Purpose* talked about learning to love their cross by which they meant to follow Christ's example and find that after sacrifice and suffering comes a new life, a getting up, a rising from the dead. They also spoke of having marriages that abided by agreed upon gender divisions. Martha had never articulated her marriage that way before but appreciated finding the words *gender divisions* to talk about the way she and Samuel had lived their lives, the words giving her a sense of dignity. The woman who seemed to be in charge, whose name was Delores, said to Martha, "Some of us go to abortion clinics on Saturday mornings to demonstrate and educate and try to save precious lives."

Martha pointed to her walker and said, "I don't want to do that. It'd be too difficult."

"I know. That's fine. But I'm wondering if you'd like to do some support work instead. You could assemble a little booklet that would tell the stories of women who had abortions and then suffered from the decision to do so. We could use it as a training tool or maybe pass it out to girls going into the clinic."

They gave her several books and pamphlets to scour; she was to choose stories that were the most affecting. As she perused the reading material, Martha was most touched by the stories of women who continued to think about the child they did not give birth to, who imagined how the child looked and behaved as each year passed. Some celebrated each of his or her birthdays (actually the date of the abortion) with a prayer or a lit candle.

She read so many of these stories and thought so long about them that she began to identify with the women who had abortions, though she herself had never had one, neither had she ever had a miscarriage. But she thought about her sixth child, the little boy she wanted to have but never did because her husband was set against the idea of having another child. She began to grieve this unborn child. She missed him as much as she missed her identical twin who had died in her mother's womb, but when she tried to imagine what he would look like, the face of the baby that Marisol had held in her arms in the church basement years before flashed before her mind as though to mock her, to mark her as ridiculous.

"Thank you for your work," Delores from *Walk with a Purpose* said one day after Martha gave her the booklet she had put together. "Now I hope you feel comfortable with our group. I hope you can open up. We tell one another *everything*. We trust one another and confide our deepest fears and problems. Such trust is part of the spiritual journey."

Martha nodded but she thought, "How can I tell them that I cannot love my cross? How can I tell them I grieve a child I never had, whom I never lost? They would think I was crazy."

At about this time, Samuel arranged to go on another trip to Rochester, Minnesota to the Mayo Clinic. Although the doctors there had previously been unable to diagnose Martha's condition, they suggested that Martha get an implant in her abdomen—a baclofen pump to administer muscle relaxants directly to the spinal cord. Though a concrete remedy eluded the Mayo doctors as much as it had local doctors, they hoped the pump would relieve Martha's symptoms enough to allow her to walk without the walker.

After their return from Minnesota, Samuel planned for her mother Zina to live in a nursing home. "Can't we wait another year?" Martha pleaded.

"How can we?" he asked. And Martha had no answer. For a long time, her mother's needs had not been properly met. Indeed, at times her 90-year-old mother ministered to Martha, rather than the other way around. She counted her mother's departure as another one of her failures, of which so many loomed as of late. She quit meditating and quit trying to lengthen time between calls when Samuel left to do an errand.

"Why aren't you attending those *Walk with Purpose* meetings any longer?" Samuel asked her one day.

"I'd rather visit my mother. She has a bad cold," Martha answered defensively (Had there been a note of accusation in Samuel's voice?). Although she did not mention it to Samuel, she felt that her *walk with purpose* was finished, had been finished ever since her children no longer needed her, ever since Samuel refused her another child, ever since Samuel took her mother away.

The baclofen pump eased Martha's startle reflex to some degree but did not improve her walking. However, in her despair, Martha began to think of the implant (the hump in her belly that the implanted pump caused) as her final pregnancy and this contortion of her imagination did give her some comfort.

Hank

Hank had good vision, better than 20-20. He could often ID shore birds and ducks without a scope. He could easily note the color of warbler feet and the underside of warbler tails as they hopped about in treetops. He could ID hawks in flight even before he rapidly lifted his binoculars to his eyes. He had excellent balance, which, over the years, he demonstrated to and practiced with Theo and Bonnie's sons. When he had taken them on hikes along the lakefront, they walked along the narrow revetments, Hank, sure-footed, leading the way. He had superb reflexes. He was strong, having regained the strength his long stay in the hospital after his brain surgery had sapped from him. He still trusted his body to keep him well, despite the brain tumor it had unexpectedly turned out.

Over the years, Hank had also enjoyed driving with the two boys, Richie and Will, playing a game that he invented for them: "What will the Hamster Brain Do Next?" The object of the game was to identify a driver on the road who drove erratically and then guess what he or she might do next. Hank used the game to teach the boys the rules of the road and to boost his own confidence in his superior driving skills. The boys loved it, being ever eager to earn Hank's approval by making an accurate prediction or proving they were aware of their surroundings— one of Hank's most stressed values and lessons.

*

One evening as Ruthie and Hank were watching the news, a story came on that discussed the first attempt to clone a primate. "I wouldn't mind being cloned," Hank said.
"You have got to be kidding. That'd be creepy," Ruthie replied.

"Why?" Hank said. "Why would it be creepy? Are you so afraid of seeing yourself?"

"I'm not even sure what you mean," Ruthie answered.

"Look," Hank said, "You could really understand and help a kid who was like you. You would know him so well and you could protect him from people who did not understand him, maybe people who did not know about dyslexia or brain surgery. You could give the poor little kid some support and encouragement. If he was the shortest kid in the class, you would know how to reassure him that he would grow with time, and you could teach him how to lift weights. And he would become strong."

Hank noticed that Ruthie did not reply. ("End of conversation," he thought.) He had not convinced her. She did not comprehend. She could not get past "creepy." He might have been surprised to learn that years later, after he had died, she would think back on the conversation and fathom its pathos, find herself awash in the plaintiveness of his strange desire.

Despite his defense of cloning, Hank knew he would never have been able to take on the responsibility of raising a child, cloned or not. His finances were always uncertain, he had a hard time saving money, and he was inspired by the feeling of freedom his job and his touch-and-go life afforded him. Taking Richie and Will on adventures had satisfied any paternal need he ever had.

"When people come from unhappy families, they seem to either want to prove they could do better and are gung-ho on having a family, or, on the other hand, want to avoid having a family altogether," Ruthie had once felt the need to explain. Ruthie fell in the latter category.

And she added with intentional exaggeration, "I find even caring for Dolly requires more emotional stamina and time than I can often muster." And yet, Hank appreciated her maternal concern that embraced the cat and him and noticed that the dynamics of families, specifically Hank's childhood family, fascinated her: she responded to Gladys's absence with the same fervor she might have directed to the absence of her own mother, who had died before she could know her.

*

"Did you ever find out what happened to your father?" Ruthie asked Hank one evening as they were working on a crossword puzzle together. "I know you told me that he was committed to a mental institution, but do you know when he died?"

"He died before I had my brain operation. My father's sister, or rather her husband, asked Felix and me if we would visit him when he was dying. Supposedly my father was asking to see us. But I never went. I think he had cancer, but I'm not sure."

"What about Felix? Did he go?"

"Bugs followed my lead."

"And Samuel?"

"*El Jefe*? I don't know about *Jefe*. I am not sure Ladimer even knew *Jefe's* phone number. *Jefe* was married by then. *Incognito*."

Hank silently noted the strange coincidence. *Incognito* answered the crossword clue, but also seemed to describe Samuel after his marriage; that is, it seemed to conclude his answer to Ruthie's question about Samuel. However, Hank said nothing about the coincidence. He pretended he was only concentrating on the daily crossword, totally indifferent to the conversation, finding her questions a mildly annoying distraction from the task at hand.

*

The evenings that they did not do a crossword puzzle together, Ruthie would read in the living room and Hank would do an advanced Sudoku in his man cave in the finished basement where he could smoke freely, or he would stare into space awhile, thinking about an unsolved math problem, such as the Birch-Tate conjecture or Hilbert's fifteenth problem. He did not even pretend he had enough knowledge or education to try to solve these problems, but he thought that maybe he could eventually understand the problems themselves. He would doodle graphs and equations on a tablet trying to formulate an understanding. On the same tablet, he would draw diagrams to visualize how he would straighten a mangled fender, a job that had just come into Scout's garage. And although he could almost always hold problems more emotional than a damaged car at bay, they seeped into his reckonings. The deaths of Theo and Bugs and Chester, and the life that his mother had chosen to live without him—these, too, counted in the recesses of his mind as he scribbled out and reshaped more practical problems, problems that could be mapped out and diagramed, with his able, intelligent hands.

*

When business slowed at Benny's shop, Hank started restoring vintage cars with his friend Scout in Scout's huge garage. Scout's garage was a hangout for neighborhood friends, gear heads, and rich old men with the money to finally own the dream cars of their youth. Scout was an ace mechanic, but he needed Hank to straighten body parts that were no longer available to buy and to prep the cars for painting, and although Hank was about twenty years older than Scout, they bonded and became a good team.

Ruthie was happy he left Benny's. She could never quite forgive Benny for the way he had treated Hank after his operation. But Hank knew she was worried about the drinking at Scout's. Ruthie's only concern was her perpetual one of late: alcohol. After work, the guys would socialize and drink, and Hank did not limit himself to one or two beers. On Saturday mornings, still in bed, Hank often heard Ruthie up and about, singing one of the songs she sang to Dolly, the cat, but he knew the not-so-subtle message was for him:

> We're coming, we're coming, our brave little band
> On the right side of temp'rance we do take our stand.
> We don't use tobacco, because we do think
> That the people who use it are likely to drink
>
> Away, away, with rum, by gum,
> Rum by gum, rum by gum
> Away, away, with rum, by gum,
> The song of the Temperance Union.

It was funny, and it was not funny. It was in the spirit of good will, and it was not in the spirit of good will. In Hank's opinion, Ruthie tended to flaunt her virtue and competency. When irritated, Hank called her "Goody Two Shoes," "Nice Nelly," and "Wowzer." She would reply ironically, "I am better than that." But she took his criticism to heart, and he knew she knew that he was not entirely off the mark. And she knew that he knew she saw him clearly and lovingly beyond daily irritations and the tribulations of addiction. He might have said she could see his soul, except he did not talk like that, nor did he want to, being an atheist and not wanting to venture near such a fraught word as *soul*.

He had been trying to moderate his drinking, but the truth was mortality mocked him of late, made faces, told grim knock-knock jokes, beckoned with insistence. Reluctantly, he was letting go of his confidence in his body's ability to outwit whatever came its way. After his MRI, Dr. Ramirez told him that the tumor was now the size of a lemon. If you thought about it, a lemon was not that much smaller than a navel orange. And although this result might have led him not to drink, even to quit smoking, anxiety led him in the opposite direction.

He noticed that his excellent vision blurred now at times or sent flashes of light. He woke up with headaches, maybe from the beer, but maybe not. He tripped and fell on the stairs one night—maybe the drinking, but maybe not. The police stopped him after dark as he was driving home from Scout's. They said his car was swaying as he drove. It sounded lame to explain he had been blinded by a flash of light emanating from his own eyes, though, true, he also had been drinking. Daily now, he felt a tumor slowly but relentlessly growing within the head within the body he had always trusted to pull him through—and new days coming, and even good days coming, meant time was passing, catching up with him.

Samuel

Samuel received a letter about his brother Hank from a woman named Ruth Winters. It explained that Hank had had to have his second brain operation for the tumor and that during the operation, he had had a stroke. The stroke had left him with some vision and cognitive and co-ordination problems. He was now recovering in a rehabilitation facility. Perhaps Samuel would like to talk to his brother? Perhaps he would like to visit him in rehab? The letter included addresses and phone numbers. Evidently Hank had been living with this woman Ruth for a number of years. They shared a home on the Southwest side of Chicago. Ruth Winters mentioned that she was in the process of converting the walk-in basement, which already had a large bathroom, to be completely handicap accessible so that Hank would be comfortable and safe when he returned home.

Samuel had not given much thought to his brother for quite some time, and indeed, chased many of the memories from his childhood away. He had been preoccupied with Martha and her illness. His mother-in-law had died. His five children had all grown up, finished college and left home, and all but Steve lived out of state. Still Martha planned trips to see them twice a year. Samuel pushed her up the ramp onto the airplane in a wheelchair. They had six grandchildren, five of who (Steve's children), lived nearby, which involved a lot of babysitting. Since Martha's coordination and balance could not be trusted, much of the looking-after fell to Samuel. An old tune filled his days—*Take good care of the baby.* Lyrics that his daughter Sophie once sang, words that had accompanied the haunting choral music of *Black Sheep.* Carefully holding small infants in his arms or bouncing toddlers or teaching the preschooler his colors comforted Samuel: the small earnest faces reaffirmed the ultimate rightness of his life's choices. Although he had retired, he was as busy as ever, monitoring investments, overseeing repairs on the house, attending to Martha, visiting children, watching grandchildren. He had a boat, which he seldom used, docked in Lake Michigan that had to be serviced twice a year. He needed to do that soon.

He didn't know if he wanted to call Hank or not. He did not want to get involved in another complicated illness, especially with someone with whom he had such a tangled, and yet estranged, relationship. Maybe this woman Ruthie expected financial help? He doubted the good sense of any woman who would choose to be with Hank. In the end he did reluctantly make the phone call. At first, Hank seemed confused about who was calling. Probably this woman Ruth had not told Hank she had written to tell Samuel what had happened, did not tell Hank that she had suggested that Samuel call. Hank seemed in a hurry to get off the phone. He was about to have a session of physical therapy. They said goodbye, and Samuel did not call him back. He told himself, "At least I tried. If they want me to do more, they can call me back."

Meanwhile, Martha's baclofen pump meant more trips to the doctor to adjust dosages and to refill the medications. And her depression and anxiety added even more medical appointments to their schedule: all the while, Samuel secretly feared she was becoming addicted to Xanax or Prozac, or both. Sometimes when he looked at Martha, he saw the beautiful woman he had married, the mother of his dear children, the woman who had helped him construct a respectable life, a crowded life, busy enough to try to fill the hole in his heart, but sometimes he saw just a body whose abdomen was distorted by an implanted pump, whose tensed legs could not support her weight, whose slurred demands seemed to stretch his penance into eternity. And when she sat in her mother's throne-like wheelchair as she did more and more often, he saw his own powerlessness before her imperial bearing. He cared for her himself, though the psychiatrist had suggested he hire a caretaker, at least part time. Martha did not want a caretaker other than him and he calculated and then balked at the expense a caretaker would involve. When the psychiatrist counseled Samuel alone, he said that maybe by overly devoting himself to his wife Martha, Samuel thought he might be able to appease his mother Gladys, make her to have never disappeared. Samuel didn't disagree. He had barely heard the psychiatrist's theory because an impossible image forming in his mind captured his attention: a void in the universe that had not been filled by his ceaseless activity, but now the void fading away, as though being erased. How can one erase a void? How can one appease an absence? He neither asked nor answered these questions with words. He just sat with the strange images in his head and a gaze of bemusement. He could not analyze why he scrambled to answer his troubled wife's every beck and call. Maybe he just did not know what else to do with his time.

A couple of years went by before he heard anything more from or about his brother. Then, on Samuel's 65th birthday, Hank called him. Hank was at home by then. He spoke to Samuel about ordinary things as though nearly 25 years without a real conversation had never even happened. In turn, Samuel told him tidbits of news about each of his children. He did not mention Martha's condition, but he told him about his boat and a fishing trip he had once taken into the wilderness of upper Canada.

"The thing with me is," Hank said, "I can't drive anymore. The vision in my left eye is shot. I don't have much peripheral vision. My left hand doesn't always do what I tell it to do. The other thing is a year or so after my brain operation, I found out I had lung cancer. They think they got it all, but all the operations have left me weak."

"You will be okay," Samuel said, hoping not to hear anymore of

Hank's troubles. Compassion wearied him these days and wasn't it so like Hank to suffer one catastrophe after another? Cancer on top of a stroke on top of a brain tumor? And, knowing Hank, he probably never quit smoking, probably drank too much. "Maybe I can pick you up sometime and we can take a ride in my boat."

"Yeah, okay," Hank said. "That would be just ducky."

When Samuel mentioned taking Hank boating, he believed he would do so. However, after he hung up, his resolve waned. He had a hard time imagining Martha's acceptance if she found out that his brother was in his life again and was going to take him from her for a whole day. As things stood, even if he just went to the store alone, Martha would text him three or four times to remind him of an item to buy, to reassure herself that he would come home. Sometimes it seemed easier just to renounce any independence, to put on the hair shirt of a martyr and try that metaphor for size and measure and fit. And so one thing led to another—busy days, busy weeks—and he never followed up with Hank. The boat sat in Burnham Harbor all summer unused.

The next time Samuel heard anything about his brother was a year later when Hank's childhood friend Arty telephoned to tell Samuel that his brother was dying. He said, "Dude, you should go say goodbye to him. He's dying." Hank's cancer had returned and spread to his liver. The word "dying" hit Samuel forcefully, finally spurring him on to visit Hank. Samuel called Ruthie at the number Arty had given him and arranged a visit.

*

Walking up to the house, Samuel noticed quirky Christmas decorations sprinkling the lawn. Stocking caps on small bushes, pinecones in red baskets, evergreen garland on the rail, a lopsided bow on a wreath on the door. Ruthie answered the bell. When he had spoken to her on the telephone, Samuel got the impression from her voice that she was quite young, so her greying hair and the smiling wrinkles around her eyes surprised him. She seemed more mature and sensible than anyone he would imagine Hank to be with. He expected the visit to be awkward. However, Ruthie seemed genuinely happy to see him and thanked him for coming. "Hank's so looking forward to seeing you," she said as she poured and handed him a cup of coffee in the small kitchen and then led the way downstairs.

Hank was sitting on the bed, and Ruthie drew up a chair and a small side table for Samuel, and then she left the two brothers to talk. They both, of course, had aged in twenty-five years and were surprised to see the older versions of each other. Hank, though dying, had a ruddy hue. His hair had not turned grey or white, but he looked fragile and unsteady. Samuel had white hair, the color of their father's hair when he walked out of his office that long-ago day, the day their mother informed them of their father's mental illness. Samuel started out on a casual note. "Hey, Hank," he said. "How are you feeling today?"

"Doing okay," Hank replied with conviction.

The conversation continued. They did not talk about Hank's impending death. They did not talk about Felix or Chester, or Gladys. They did not talk about Martha or her illness or the ruptures in Samuel and Hank's fraternal relationship. Samuel told Hank about his children and grandchildren, and Hank told his brother, whom he still called *Jefe*, about Theo and Bonnie's children and the adventures he had shared with them. They talked a bit about fishing. Hank told *Jefe* a few things about learning to bird. He also told him about studying the buildings downtown with Ruthie, mentioning that that was how they had met. Hank seemed fairly lucid as he spoke, though sometimes he got confused about a name or time period; sometimes he slurred his words or mispronounced them. Both had a lifetime of hurt that needed to be voiced, but neither's lips could steer the conversation toward the words that needed to be said.

When their conversation started to wane, Samuel fetched Ruthie upstairs, asking her to take a photo of him and Hank with his smart phone. Then Samuel took a photograph of Ruthie and Hank sitting on the bed, next to each other with Ruthie's arm around Hank's shoulder, the same pose Samuel had struck with Hank. Ruthie asked Samuel to email her copies of the photographs, and she went upstairs to see if they had arrived on her computer. Through all of their adventures together and despite her artistic work with photographs, she and Hank hardly ever took photographs of themselves. Maybe because of her critical scrutiny of photographs as she reworked them in her art work, she felt superstitious and wary of capturing time, of overshadowing experience. But now that she knew Hank would soon be gone, she welcomed Samuel's offer to photograph them together. Soon Samuel followed her upstairs.

They spoke awhile about Hank's illness. After detailing all Hank had been through and what one doctor said and then what another doctor said, Ruthie apologized for babbling. "It's just that I've had no one to talk to about this," she said. "It weighs heavy sometimes."

"There's no need to apologize at all," said Samuel. "He's lucky to have you to care for him at home."

"Unfortunately, I'm quite sure that is not true," said Ruthie. "I make a lot of mistakes. I've absolutely no medical training. I'm always so busy trying to catch up, thinking about what I need to do, I've almost no time to visit with Hank, you know, to ask him how it feels to know that he's dying. I often lose patience; I lose my temper. When I do have extra time, I wander the yard alone in a daze, decorating for Christmas like a deranged Martha Stewart. It's the only thing that relaxes me. I can't concentrate enough to read or write or draw."

Samuel listened patiently, smiling to himself. She ended by saying, "I'm so grateful that you came to visit him. I know it means a lot to him."

Samuel and Ruthie looked at each other curiously. Although they were taking measure of each other, they felt a connection as they conversed. Samuel asked if he could visit again. He suddenly felt he needed to return to this oddly ordered house bedecked with cheerful Christmas trimmings belying sickness and sorrow. More needed to be said, and perhaps Ruthie could make it easier for the brothers to talk.

"Anytime," Ruthie said. "We're here all of the time. I was able to take time off work, so I could be here with Hank." Samuel told her that he looked forward to visiting again, visiting both Hank and her, but it never happened. Within two weeks' time, Hank was dead.

Part Four: Ever After
(2015 – onward)

Who were they to say the name of the wind that had blown her away?
Maybe all they could do now was mourn.

Ruthie

The third day after Hank's death, Ruthie finally left the house. She had spent most of the three preceding days catching up on sleep, daydreaming, writing in a journal, though she had a few practical tasks to accomplish as well: calling Atwood Medical Supplies to pick up the hospital bed, and emailing the printer to have memory cards, announcing Hank's death, made up, and rearranging the furniture in the living room, which had served as a final sick room, a death room, where Hank had lain semiconscious in a hospital bed, where she had slept on the couch, up every three hours to administer lorazepam and morphine, where their old cat Dolly had rested on the rug near the electric fireplace which roared with comforting flames to match comforting music Ruthie played from Pandora on her computer. She requested Jethro Tull and Elton John, two of Hank's favorites, from Pandora's menu. Then she requested folk music and classic rock. *American Pie* kept recurring—lyrics about "good old boys" who drive Chevys and drink whiskey and rye and sing and die.

Had all the music and the fire and her watchfulness comforted Hank in the end? His legs had been restless for two days, causing him to traverse the hospital bed, scooting with his legs, tangling the sheets, and ending up in contorted, unsafe positions that Ruthie struggled to straighten out. She then had taken to massaging his legs, teasingly calling them "troublemaker legs," in an effort to still his unease and keep his head where it belonged, on the pillow at the head of the bed where she could wet his dried lips with a small sponge and drop drops of morphine under his tongue from an eye dropper, the way Bonnie, on one of her visits, had demonstrated. Hank's death had brought Ruthie and

Bonnie together in mutual sympathy, which proved to be stronger and more lasting than any lingering jealousy. Bonnie's oldest son Richie paid the greatest tribute to Hank months later at a memorial picnic:

"I knew Hank for my entire life. He came late to my christening, though he was my godfather and should have come early to practice his role. He came late because he stopped on the way to play craps and win 500 dollars for my gift to start me off right in this world. He had a quality that not many people have and that is an appreciation for life. Whether this came from his battles with illness or just from his natural personality, I could never figure out. Hank lived his life without fear of rules or the need to fit in. He knew life was short and he was going to live it to the fullest.

"Hank was an explorer and a maker. Many times, he would take my brother and me on hikes through the forest preserves and the first thing he would want to do was go off the beaten path. A few times we got seriously lost, but that was okay—to Hank that was the fun part. He loved to tinker and make things as well. He was always building some new car or trying to learn some new skill. His thirst for knowledge was never-ending. He probably has been to every museum in Chicago. Did you know there was a hologram museum in Chicago, because Hank did, and it was amazing. He taught me to pay attention to my surroundings and to be a good driver. He made me practice balancing as we walked over rocks on the beach, and with my father he taught me how to play football and moonwalk on roller skates.

"So as we think of Hank today, I ask that we try to live a little more like him, seeing past the mundane shadows of life and exploring the true light the wonders of this world can hold for us."

*

The days before his death, Hank's restlessness subsided: he was quiet but breathing so laboriously that he awoke Ruthie when she dozed off. She called hospice about the breathing, and was told to give more morphine, more lorazepam, not to be afraid to give too much. He wore a fentanyl patch for pain in addition to the medications she dropped under his tongue. He died later that afternoon. The hospice nurse came to wash his body and make the final arrangements for the donation of his body to medicine.

But now all of that was over. A heavy burden lifted. At first, the overwhelming feeling was just pure relief. No more medicine to administer. No more sheets or bedclothes to change. No need to move him or straighten him out. No more worry that she was doing something wrong or that he was uncomfortable or in pain or scared. No more worry that he might fall. No more worry about how it would all end because now it had all ended: the incredible heaviness of being—and now the incredible lightness.

That relief marked the first day after he died, a day during which she had stayed in bed staring at the ceiling when not dozing. The second day she slowly made her way from her bed to an easy chair with her laptop in tow. She sent the memory-card file to the print shop and then put the computer on the floor and paused to take in the absence. Dolly jumped on her lap. Hank's body had been picked up by a medical service and brought to a morgue the day he died. It would be used for medical research (touting their confidence in science, they both had signed up years before) and then cremated. She would receive the ashes in a few months. She would send the cards. She would create a virtual memorial. She would host a memorial picnic in the summer. She started a "to do" list, often pausing to stare out in space. Space seemed holy. Her solitariness and the quiet around her seemed holy. The simple things she touched—the teapot, the doorknob, the cord to open the drapes—seemed holy. Her hand touched what his hand had once touched, imprints fusing.

Sadness finally found its place side by side with reflection and relief. She rifled through his belongings—a set of keys, a pair of binoculars, a pocket knife—each one silent, each one remaining after him, oblivious to his momentous absence. She picked up one of his Sudoku books and leafed through it, seeing only half of the puzzles completed, remembering how after the stroke, he no longer could do advanced Sudoku puzzles. Sometimes they had tried to do a simple one together, but the numbers, once his friends, his helpers, simply would not behave, they danced crazily with jointed cartoon legs in his head, so he chased them away and closed the puzzle book. She had kept hoping to hear some deathbed revelation from him, some resolution that would offer enlightenment to a troubled life, but she eventually realized that death with its pain and confusion did not lead to meaning. It clouded more than clarified. His lips offered no final words of wisdom, no epiphany.

During his final years, he had stayed almost all day in his basement hideout watching television, or, if the weather was good, he would shuffle out to the garage to repeatedly organize and reorganize the tools and supplies he kept there. He gave his fishing lures away to Theo and Bonnie's now grown sons. Sometimes he would take walks around the neighborhood. Though in pain, he did not let go of the future. He hoped modestly. Maybe he would eventually be able to drive again or maybe work.

The third day after Hank's death, Ruthie ventured out of the house to walk to the print shop to pick up the cards; she walked still swathed in an aura of the sacred, each step sacred, her senses attuned to significance. A block on her way, a white cat suddenly appeared on the sidewalk ahead, a cat she had never seen before—and she knew all the cats around the neighborhood very well, having given each of them a special name. The white cat waited for her to catch up, meowing. She could see that it was hungry. "Spirit Cat," she called to it. It walked up to her and wound around her legs. She turned around and started walking back home to fetch it some of Dolly's kibble. The cat followed her, meowing. At one point, Ruthie stopped and picked it up to comfort it and then carried it the rest of the way. The strange cat offered no resistance, waited by the back door while Ruthie went inside to grab some of Dolly's dried food and a few cat treats. The strange white cat ate the food Ruthie offered. When it finished eating, Ruthie sat down on the back stoop and petted it for a while, calling it by its new name, "Spirit." "How are you doing my dear Old Friend?" she asked, fussing over her new "Old" Friend. She thought of her long-ago conversation with Hank about the bright star signaling Felix's death. Messages and messengers infuse the world when we are receptive enough to listen for them or see them or name them or perhaps imagine them, she thought. She finally left the cat, full and content, on her stoop, hoping it would still be there when she returned from the print shop. However, when she got back, it was nowhere to be found, though she called and called for it. After its brief and ghostly appearance, she never saw it again.

Bonnie

Bonnie is holding Hank's hand as she sits next to his hospital bed
in the living room of his house. Her knitting is in a bag at her feet
and on a chair is a copy of *The Adventures of Tom Sawyer*. She had
hunted for it in the basement before she came, having remembered
that once in grade school she had read it to him as they sat on the
floor together. Hank had been very impressed with her reading ability. But with this particular book, it was not only her reading ability
that held his attention. For the rest of his life he would allude to
whitewashing the fence—he had loved that con-job part in the book.
He would sometimes say years later, "I did a Tom Sawyer on him."
Bonnie picks up the book and reads the passage:

> "Does a boy get a chance to whitewash a fence every day?"
> That put the thing in a new light....
> "Say, Tom, let me whitewash a little."
> Tom considered, was about to consent; but he altered his mind:
> "No—no—I reckon it wouldn't hardly do, Ben. You see, Aunt
> Polly's awful particular about this fence—right here on the street,
> you know."

As Bonnie reads, she hopes to put a smile on her unconscious
friend's face. But Hank continues to sleep, expressionless. She puts
down the book, and picks up her knitting: "knit, purl, knit, purl,
purl."

Ruthie is at the bank. She needed someone to stay with Hank.
Ruthie and Bonnie have formed an alliance now—any residue of

wariness has gone. All that matters now is Hank. Hank is dying. Bonnie has shown Ruthie how to change bedding and diapers, how to cut a slit down the back of Hank's t-shirts, so she can dress him more easily. She has asked and answered questions with her, taken from hospice's *Book of Comfort*:

What are the signs of death?
What will breathing be like?
What happens to the skin?
What if he stops eating?
Why is he making those odd hand gestures?
Will medication keep him pain-free?
Can he hear me?

Bonnie thinks again, *Hank is dying*. She remembers the answer to *What will breathing be like? The Book of Comfort* offers a description:

Most deaths will not be sudden. The dying will linger. Their breathing ebbs and flows, waxes and wanes, comes and goes, and finally, slowly, very slowly, the breathing stops.

Bonnie has never been a hospice nurse, though for a while she organized home nursing care for those leaving the hospital, some going home to die. She sat with her mother when she died. She sat with her father when he died. She sat with her husband Theo when he died, after she had allowed the plug to be pulled. *The Book of Comfort* explains that the dying will be visited by their loved ones who have died before them. They will come to welcome the dying person to his or her new home in the afterlife. Bonnie imagines Gladys coming to Hank to explain her long absence. Gladys does not ask for forgiveness. She merely smiles and the smile, as mysterious as that of the *Mona Lisa,* erases all pain and goes beyond evil and beyond good and beyond time, imbued with love. Bonnie imagines Felix coming, his crooked smile. He carries a large fish on a line. He is barefoot and all golden and aglow, a gladdened spirit. Bonnie imagines Theo coming. He is on roller skates, his shoulder askew. Hadn't she jerked the bones in her husband's shoulder back in place correctly? She imagines Hank and Theo skating at the rink together: a graceful dance. She thinks she might be seeing now a slight smile, a bare hint of a smile, on Hank's face as he sleeps in the hospital bed next to her. She wets his lip with a small sponge on a stick.

She puts her knitting down and picks up *The Adventures of Tom Sawyer* again. She looks for the passage where Tom and his friends attend their own funeral:

> …the congregation rose and stared while the three dead boys came marching up the aisle, Tom in the lead, Joe next, and Huck, a ruin of drooping rags, sneaking sheepishly in the rear! They had been hid in the unused gallery listening to their own funeral sermon!
>
> Aunt Polly, Mary, and the Harpers threw themselves upon their restored ones, smothered them with kisses and poured out thanksgivings….
>
> Suddenly the minister shouted at the top of his voice: "Praise God from whom all blessings flow—sing!—and put your hearts in it!"

And then Bonnie begins to sing for Hank. She sings "You Are My Sunshine," and she sings "With a Little Help from My Friends." Then Ruthie comes home and Bonnie's concert, which has been an act of love, a bit off key, is over.

Samuel

After his brother Hank died, Samuel remembered that his brother had given him his nickname, *El Jefe*, and had helped his mother bail him out of jail when he had been arrested for shooting his gun near the expressway. He remembered that he and Hank had once curled up together on Hank's bed as their mother told them stories—a comforting physicality that involved tangled limbs and clean sheets and the pleasant, earnest voice of his mother searching for the truth in a tale. Samuel also found himself thinking about all that he and Hank had failed to discuss the day he visited his dying brother, and he found himself thinking of Ruthie. Should he call her? Of course, he would see her at the memorial picnic she planned for the coming summer, but that was a few months away, and he might not get a chance to talk with her alone. He had questions he wanted to ask her. So when she e-mailed him about spreading Hank's ashes at a preserve where Hank had birded, he immediately said he would meet her, telling Martha only that he had to attend his brother's funeral. Ruthie was waiting for him at the picnic table under the shelter when he arrived at Portage. They recognized each other instantly and waved from a distance. "I have some questions to ask you," he said as he approached.

*

"I have a hard time understanding why you were with my brother," he began. "Hank was so, Hank was such a ..."

"He was a character," Ruthie finished his thought. And they both laughed. "I'm an independent character too," Ruthie said. "We got along well together."

Samuel looked puzzled. She struck him as sophisticated and refined, the opposite of his brother.

"Hank always was interested in something and kept me interested too. Hank was so smart!"

"I know he was smart, but not always on track. You never could count on him. You know about our family? Our mother? Our father? You know we did not come from a normal family?" Samuel tried to steady his voice as he spoke.

"I know, I know," Ruthie said, touching his hand to reassure him. He was broaching a difficult topic, but she seemed to welcome his sudden need to talk, to articulate what had needed to be articulated for years between the brothers. Words spilled from his mouth as though she were a confessor, or perhaps a medium, provider of a space where the living brother could commune with the dead brother —or perhaps *brothers*, for he wanted to know what Ruthie knew about Felix. He almost started crying when he remembered being told about the drowning and his refusal to get involved.

Samuel told her that since Gladys had deserted them, he and Hank had never discussed her. He traced his split with Hank back to her leaving. It had changed everything, he said. He spoke critically of Hank's lack of responsibility, but Ruthie listened silently while he was speaking, welcoming the confidences, even though she wanted to defend Hank. When she spoke up for Hank, Samuel listened too, admitting that basically he had always liked Hank, but that circumstances had led him toward a different path. "When my mother left," he said, "all I could think about was how I would survive."

"Of course," Ruthie said.

As Ruthie spoke of Hank's knowledge of the downtown buildings and his ability to bird by sound as well as sight, Samuel felt as though he were hearing about someone he did not know. He responded by telling her about his wife and family, feeling suddenly self-conscious that she might find him a bit strait-laced and conventional. She showed him the ashes that had come in the mail. Med Cure Whole Body Donation had arranged the cremation after they finished their research.

White sand. Which part of his brother did each grain represent? "Oh, Brother," Samuel thought, echoing the title of a popular movie, "Where Art Thou?"

They spread the ashes in two places that Ruthie said Hank favored: one near the bridge and one near the lookout. Samuel's phone kept vibrating. Martha needed his attention. Samuel told Ruthie about Martha's illness as he checked messages.

"I believe in commitment," he said in a solemn tone, and Ruthie listened to his words, because they seemed hard earned and important for him to say. He said the words slowly, as though he were explaining to and trying to convince not only her but himself why he so believed in commitment. It occurred to Ruthie that he did not mention, or perhaps realize, the connections to his past: Gladys had not completed her commitment to him. "I'm glad my brother found you," he told Ruthie. "But I have lived a fulfilling life too." The words seemed to come from some ancient rivalry he and Hank had lived by. Irrationally, he remembered the ice cream his mother bought for Hank when he had his tonsils removed. He was not sure from where his protest came, but they left a somewhat puzzled expression on Ruthie's face.

Always the conversation circled back to Gladys. Ruthie told him all she had found on the Internet search and all she could remember Hank saying about her. She told him about Gladys' ride to Florida with Hank. This was startling news to Samuel who didn't know where she had gone or how. Hank had never told him.

The two lingered, talking by their cars. They had so much to say that it seemed they would be able to confide in each other forever. Before they said goodbye, Ruthie said, "I wished I'd reached out earlier to you. You'd have been able to see more of Hank."

"Yes. I should've reached out when you wrote me that letter. And you and I would've been able to visit too," Samuel said.

He saw her once again at the memorial picnic. He seemed distracted when he arrived; it had been hard to get away. Martha kept insisting that going to the funeral had been enough. His phone rang on the drive over and vibrated the whole time he was there. The picnic with music and food and games and many friends meant he did not have the chance to talk in a confidential way to Ruthie that day. When they said goodbye, Ruthie said, "We had such an intense conversation the day we spread the ashes. Please do stay in touch." Samuel said he would, but in a regretful tone. He wanted to stay in touch, but probably would not be able to. His tone offered the first clue: she might not see him again. He was all too familiar with willful commitment. He accepted but resented its power to override desire and shut down possibility.

Caleb

At nine o'clock that evening, Caleb was sitting in a chair in his living room, swaying and snapping his fingers to the Latin song, "No lo Trates" by the trio Pitbull, Daddy Yankee and Natti Natasha, with lyrics begging for honesty in relationships. Then a bit later, an abrupt change in musical taste, he listened to a lively *La Bamba*. He could no longer practice dance steps due to his being a sorry gimp, and he missed the mastery his feet once flaunted: nonetheless, he sang of graceful dancing feet. His partner, Wash, was out campaigning for Maria Hadden, a queer black woman, who was running to unseat the current alderman, Joe Moore, in the Rogers Park neighborhood in Chicago where they lived. Usually Caleb would be canvassing with him, but he had had to work overtime and got home late that evening, so he was unwinding from the tensions of the day.

> *Para bailar la bamba se necesita una poca de gracia*
> *Yo no soy marinero*
> *Yo no soy marinero, soy capitán*

> To dance the bamba it takes a little grace
> I'm not a sailor
> I am not a sailor, I am a captain.

And after *La Bamba*, he listened to a recording of Handel's choral music that Wash liked.

*

Caleb worked in a small shop in the neighborhood, fixing computers. He had not seen or spoken to his father in over two years. His father had asked him not to call as his phone calls upset his wife, Martha. He was not even supposed to call his father's cell phone lest Martha be nearby. For a while, he had emailed or texted his father regularly, but even that correspondence had subsided, as Samuel's short, polite messages saddened Caleb. His half brothers and sisters, whom he met when he stayed with his father for a few months after his military service, never contacted him or indicated in any way that they wanted anything to do with him.

"At least my mother would be proud of me," he mused. Wash had sparked the political activist in him that his mother always had hoped for—*Caleb, a spy for Aztlan!* He regularly attended the local meetings of Network 49, a progressive ward organization that was fighting hard to boost Maria's chances of winning the local election. Unlike his mother, though, he always canvassed with either Wash or someone else from his group, never alone.

Wash, who worked in rehab as a massage therapist, would massage Caleb's deformed foot when he got home from campaigning, as he did most nights. Caleb still walked with a cane, but his hobbled gait had improved, thanks to the exercises Wash prescribed and the healing hands Wash laid on his foot and the soothing, optimistic words he often whispered about their future together in the neighborhood, especially once Maria won, as she surely was showing she could do. *The Promised Land.*

When the singing faded to an end, Caleb opened his laptop computer. He had started last night searching for *Hank Stone.* He remembered the name from his father's visit at the time of his graduation from high school. Samuel had told him that, like him, his brother Hank had trouble reading, but liked to fix things and was good at math. Caleb himself was not especially good at math, but he did like to fix things.

Since his military experience had exposed him to loud explosions, he was not as quick at problem solving as he had once been, but he still could troubleshoot and work with his hands. He was not even sure why he was searching for Hank Stone. Maybe in Hank, he might find someone who would include him in a paternal family.

As he continued his computer search, he found a *Hank Stone* who lived on the Southwest side of Chicago and had a landline telephone number. When he called the number, a woman answered. She told him that Hank Stone had recently died. Her name was Ruthie Winters and, in a polite, welcoming voice, she wondered if she could help him.

Gladys, Caleb and Ruthie

When her children were young, Gladys told them a story. Part of the story had been passed down from her mother, part she had learned in school, and part she had composed in her head. *A woman who was really a bird longed to return to her own creatures and her own land, a land without discord. Some days this woman hid in a closet and sewed blankets made from feathers, leaving her husband and children to fend for themselves, telling them not to disturb her, for she needed her solitude. But one of her little boys, a mischievous tot named Rabbit, peeked in the closet one day. He saw a bleeding bird, plucking its own feathers from its breast. Little Rabbit began to cry, and his tears pierced his mother's heart.* The story then took many unpredictable twists and turns, and each time was a bit different and continued and continued for however long it took a child to fall asleep.

When she told the tale to Felix, he cried when the mother flew away to her own land to live with her own creatures. Gladys told him, "The mother was never as happy there as she thought she might be." Gladys kept trying to make the story end happily to cheer Felix up. She made up a part in which the children too began to grow wings and feathers. But in the end that was of little comfort, for Felix did not want to be a bird. Gladys' abilities fell short when it came to happy endings.

*

Caleb and Ruthie stood before a columbarium in the cemetery in Davie, Florida, the cemetery mentioned in Gladys' obituary, the place where the urn with Gladys's ashes was kept. When Caleb and Ruthie first met in person, their conversations were mostly about Samuel and Martha and Marisol.

"My father's wife keeps him on a very short leash," Caleb told Ruthie one of the first times they conversed. "She's very possessive. I know she's ill and all, but as far as I can tell, she was like that even before she got sick." Caleb thought then of how he had had to keep to himself for the short time he stayed in Martha's house. She had never invited him to eat with the family. He said, "She wanted to create a world of her own with that large family in its McMansion. Samuel's job was to make money to keep the whole shebang going." Caleb always thought with resentment that Samuel would see him more often if he could do so without upsetting Martha, but Caleb knew to be fair he shouldn't blame Martha entirely. Somehow Samuel felt safe being tied to her, taking care of her. Samuel was the one who should have defended him, made sure he was included.

"I 've always been wary of families," Ruthie told him. "I didn't come from a normal happy family and neither did Hank. I've always thought of families in the same way as I think of closed circles. They include and exclude at the same time. I've always felt more comfortable hovering about the circle than being in it. It's weird, but Samuel is making us feel a small bit of what he must have felt when his mother left."

"When I was a kid, I always wanted a family with a mother and father," Caleb said simply.

Inevitably, their early conversations turned to Gladys and the mystery of her disappearance. Ruthie told Caleb the bits and pieces of what she knew, and he told her that Gladys had always been kind to his mother Marisol when she was a little girl living in the apartment above. "My mother told me that Gladys took her in her arms once to comfort her when some neighborhood toughs followed her home from school, threatening to cut her braids." Both Caleb and Ruthie looked forward to these conversations, as though they were on a spiritual journey together, one that honored memory. Even if the memory was scarred and sketchy and not their own, they came to regard it as a moral imperative to reveal and protect it. One day, Caleb hunted for a letter he thought he still might have somewhere. In an old duffel bag, he found his mother's ring, the one she told him Gladys had asked her to keep, and the letter that Gladys had written and the photograph card that Samuel had given him at his high school graduation. When he showed Ruthie the card, a chill ran through her. The photograph of Samuel's family all fair and smiling and perfect reminded her of the photographs she ironically touched up in her artwork. Caleb gave the ring to Ruthie to try on, but in the end, it fit his pinky finger perfectly and so they decided he should wear it. They would wonder about its symbolism later, but at that moment Ruthie eagerly turned to the letter. She and Caleb combed the letter for information. "The address," she said. "If your mom had told Hank or Samuel the address, they could have found her, brought her back or at least visited her in Florida."

At a certain point as Ruthie and Caleb talked, the idea hatched of going to the cemetery where Gladys was buried to see if they could find out more or maybe just feel a better connection with the mystery. Before the trip, Ruthie reviewed the material she had found on the Internet a long time before. She reread the obituaries and revisited the social security site. She wrote everything she knew on a note pad, including, most significantly, the address from Marisol's letter. She made a sketchy timeline with the little bit of information that she had gathered.

Caleb and Ruthie took a cab from the Hollywood-Ft. Lauderdale airport to Davie and drove past the address found on the letter. Gladys sent Marisol. But whatever had once stood there on Franklin Street was now gone. They found a strip mall, which stood where they had hoped to find a house or an apartment building. At the cemetery, they tried to find out as much as they could by questioning the caretaker and the clerk in the office who was willing to look up records and scour files. They learned that Gladys herself had paid for the cremation a few months ahead of time. She had written the obituary and left directions for the death date to be added and for it to be printed in the paper both in Fort Lauderdale and in Miami. A notation remained, then, in those places for anyone who might want to find out in future years that she had, indeed, once existed: a meager legacy for her children. The trip to the cemetery crystalized a story about Gladys that had been forming in Ruthie's mind. She told her version of the story to Caleb:

When Gladys left Cicero with Hank that March day in 1969, she only had a vague idea that she might be leaving for good. She had felt herself in danger for a long time. The danger hovered in the house that she was leaving and stemmed from Chester's mental illness, from Ladimer's sinister presence, and from her own instability. Riding down to Florida with Hank and his friends, she felt incredibly liberated. She led the boys in song and told them stories of her childhood in South Dakota. But the jubilance was short lived. When they arrived at the racetrack in Florida and as she made arrangements with Hank to pick her up at the end of the week, the thought of returning was already starting to dampen her spirits and frighten her. A familiar knot in her gut—one she had known since childhood—tightened.

She knew several people from Hawthorne racetrack who now worked at Gulfstream. Perhaps she even had a lover there, though not anyone she was desperate to see or that she would leave her children for—just someone with whom she could pass the time, someone who could help her assess her chances of making a go of it in Florida on her own, for that vague idea of leaving seemed clearer now, and pressing. She pushed the consequences out of her mind. She would not have been able to bear the thought of permanently leaving her children, especially her youngest, Felix, who needed her still.

Finding a job was not difficult. Maybe if she had not found one so readily, within a day or two, she would not have stayed. But things fell in place so effortlessly. She tended bar well. She was personable and still pretty. These abilities and traits eased the way.

Working at her new job at a racetrack bar, she had been nervous and jumpy the whole day she knew she was supposed to meet Hank to go home, her mind flashing an image of him anxiously waiting for her at the entrance gate, but her gut churning at the thought of running out to meet him to go back—to go back now—seemed a death sentence.

She did call Felix on his birthday a few weeks later and cried afterward, unable to understand or forgive herself.

Work was her salvation. She worked long hours, always eager to work an extra shift. Her future floated obscurely before her. It included a vague idea that Samuel or Hank would find her someday and they would welcome and redeem her and include her once again in a family circle. But for now, her fear of Ladimer kept her from calling home. She did not want him to find out where she was. As months and then years went by, shame prevented her from reconnecting. So unlike her independent self, she sometimes indulged in comforting fantasy: a maiden in distress, rescued by her strapping sons. She had asked for secrecy in the letter she had sent Marisol, but maybe she really hoped for revelation. She confided in no one at work. She had no real friends, though she kept cordial relations. Sometimes the sunny days and warm weather buoyed her spirits, offering a humble reprieve.

In a story that her mother once told of the man who lived with two battling wolves within him, one of the wolves was regret and alienation and one was joy and community. The wolf who would be victorious would be the one the man fed and nurtured. Gladys was quite sure she didn't have that much control over the battling wolves within her. Which to feed and nurture was not her choice.

Years passed. At the public library she found books of folktales to read. She may have even tried to sort out the origins and variations of the tales she had told her sons, using the tales to try to ground herself. On the library computer she learned to search for her children. She could not find very much about Hank or Felix, but it seemed that Samuel was married. Maybe she had grandchildren? Even that joyful thought probably ended in disappointment, for she felt undeserving, and she knew she would never be able to see them if, indeed, they existed. She had given up on her daydream rescue and felt too humiliated at such a late date to make herself known to the sons she had deserted. Death now would be welcome, would save her from waking up another morning to face the enormity of her transgression.

Caleb listened carefully to Ruthie's story, but he had ideas of his own. He said, "I think she may have left because she was pregnant and did not want her baby to be in danger—I mean, you know, Chester and his illness, Ladimer and the mob. She was still young enough then to have a baby."

Ruthie smiled, not finding Caleb's version very credible and feeling hesitant to give up her own narrative. "Well, at least in your version, she would not carry as heavily the taboo of being a bad mother," she conceded. But then she suddenly felt impatient, not just with Caleb, but with their entire pilgrimage. Why were they here now in the middle of a tangled plot that they had made their own, with no possible resolution? Who were they to say the name of the wind that had blown her away? Maybe all their guesses about her were wrong.

"When one person disappears mysteriously, the whole world seems dim and silent," Ruthie thought.

Ruthie suddenly was reminded of the day she told Hank what she had learned about Gladys' death on her Internet search and how he had ignored her report as though he knew that details and information could no longer touch the depths of his darkness or add to understanding the secrets of the human heart. Ever since he first grasped the concept of randomness in first grade, Hank had accepted that human comportment defied logic and belied the facts: Sherlock Holmes, except in stories, would never have been able to solve a mystery.

Ruthie thought to herself, "No one is here to pull the thorn from the heart," though her sentiment embraced everyone and everything and all time and was not necessarily related to Samuel's absence. The brothers had learned to live beyond the hope their mother would ever return to them. And yet Hank, until the very end, even just weeks before he died, hoped he would be able to drive an automobile again someday, hoped he would be able to go back to work in Scout's garage. A few days before he died, when it had seemed obvious to Ruthie that he would die presently, he asked her to buy him some new socks because all of his old ones were no longer white and snug, but faded, stretched and ragged.

Joyce Goldenstern writes and lives by fiction, often inspired by folk tales, animals, visual art, and other literature as well as her own experiences. She has published a collection of short stories, *The Story Ends—The Story Never Ends*, and two chapbooks, *Old Woman and Eel and Other Prose Pieces* and *Way Stops Americana,* as well as five nonfiction children's books. She has received two Illinois Arts Council awards, a Quarterly West Novella Contest award, and a Chicago Council of Fine Arts Neighborhood Workshop grant. She lives in Chicago. Her website is https://thestoryendsthestoryneverends.wordpress.com/.